CW01429067
EMPIRE

Fallen EMPIRE

Empire Nightclub #4

K.A. TUCKER

ISBN 978-1-990105-48-7 (Ingram paperback edition)
ISBN 978-1-990105-03-6 (KDP paperback edition)
ISBN 978-1-990105-12-8 (ebook edition)

Editing by Hot Tree Editing

Cover design by Shanoff Designs

Published by K.A. Tucker Books Ltd.

ONE
GABRIEL

"WELL, would you look at that. I'll bet you thought you had that hand in the bag." Caleb grins as he lays down a straight flush beside Cohen's four aces. "Oh wait, *you* bet. *A lot.*"

With a curse under his breath, the owner of the Mage Hotel and Casino sinks into his chair and scowls as his opponent rakes in the considerable pot of chips. Has he figured out yet that my brother's been stringing him along, like a lion toying with its meal before going in for the kill? He allowed the little bald man to win five hands out of six, enough to nurture the delusion that Caleb is all talk and no skill. The growing number of chips tossed onto the table with each round is proof of it.

But Caleb isn't known for having patience and is tiring of this ruse. He leans back in his chair, stretching his arms behind his head. "Come on, Gabe. You ready to jump in and lose to me too?"

"Not this round." I reject his taunt with an unbothered drawl. I've never been able to play poker with him. He's an arrogant prick on a regular day, but put him in a Vegas high-roller room? My fist is itching to connect with his jaw and my money's not even in play.

Besides, my head's not on the game. It's barely processing the swanky room or the armed security detail loitering around us. It's still in the hotel lobby, on the phone, listening to our private eye Stanley inform me that it wasn't our dear uncle Peter who rigged our private jet to explode two nights ago. It wasn't even our family nemesis, the now-deceased Camillo Perri, or his two equally deceased sons.

Our father's henchman was the one lurking within the range of a security camera the night we nearly died, and Bane only takes orders from one man.

Our father.

I understand what Stanley was trying to tell me over that phone call, but I'm still struggling to process it. No one has ever accused Vlad Easton of being loving, but to sic his homicidal dog on us like that?

The air in the room is tense as the dealer distributes fresh hands.

"So, when are we gonna start playing like real men?" Caleb rearranges his cards with the stony expression he's mastered. For all the swagger he throws around, not many can outmatch his poker face.

"Real men play with deep pockets. What do you have in your pockets that I might want, Mr. *Easton*?" Cohen peers over his hand with a glint in his eye that makes me wonder if maybe he's been playing us all along, too. At least he spent five seconds researching his opponent before he sat down in that chair, long enough to know who Mr. Green *really* is. But we've done plenty of digging on Bruce Cohen and we know he's a sneeze away from losing his hold of this hotel thanks to his penchant for prostitutes and blow, and making terrible decisions in this very room.

Does it bother Cohen that he's sitting across from the son of a notorious crime boss? Is he worried what will happen if he upsets us? Nah…. This little man may be a degenerate gambler on the verge of economic collapse, but he's dealt with his share of shady fucks. He knows exactly who we are, and I suspect he can guess how much we're worth.

A ballpark guess, anyway. Nobody has an actual idea except our accountant, who has made sure to bury that number where no one will ever find it.

"Where to begin…," Caleb drawls, sucking back a mouthful of vodka. I fight the urge to cringe. It's ten a.m. "How about a lucrative nightclub in Phoenix—"

"That's not on the table." I glare at my older brother. If this is his go-big-or-go-home strategy, I'd rather go home. The club is half mine and Caleb can only work so much magic if he gets a shitty hand.

"Ye of little faith." Caleb smirks. "Fine, little brother. What do you suggest I risk losing in this respectable game to this respectable gentleman?"

"A few apartment buildings," I say without hesitation. Our father's properties, safely tucked away under dear Aunt Vespa's name—Dad and Uncle Pete's older sister who suffers from dementia and is riding out her days in a deluxe old-age home, convinced it's still 1954.

Caleb has power of attorney and deals with the property manager.

Caleb's blue eyes flash to mine, and a curious frown zags across his forehead. I know what he's thinking: that Dad would kill us if Caleb lost those assets in a game of poker. But considering he's already given the order to kill us, I guess that's a moot point. Not that Caleb knows about that small detail yet.

But Vlad Easton didn't *actually* intend to kill his sons, did he? If that was the goal, Bane would have waited until we were snug in our seats before he flipped the trigger. No.... That display had to be a warning: be good little sons, fall in line for big bad Vlad. Now that he's behind bars until the end of his days, he's hellbent on seeing his delightful *legacy*—a drug empire—continue on in this world, with us taking it over. We've avoided and sidestepped the dirtiest parts of the family business up until now. He thinks he can scare us into compliance.

That, or he's being a spiteful prick and wants to piss us off. If that's the case, he has succeeded in the latter. Caleb's liable to choke the last few years out of him on the spot when he hears about this.

But how pissed is Dad going to be when he finds out his grand plan of an alliance with the Perris to ward off the cartel will never happen, now that three out of five Perris are dead and the other two are as eager to carry on their family's illicit business as we are?

"And what could I possibly want with apartment buildings? I assume in Phoenix, no less," Cohen asks, shifting his cards around in his hand.

Yeah, he's definitely done some homework on us.

Cohen smooths a palm over his shiny forehead as he studies his cards with a puckered frown. He has a terrible poker face. With just the hands I've watched, I can tell he has a flush of some sort and he's going to pretend he doesn't. No wonder the guy is up to his eyeballs in debt that he's forged at this table.

"It's not the buildings per say, but the property. They're Scottsdale prime real estate. Developers are knocking on our door every week." Caleb folds his hand in a tidy bundle, thumbs crossed. To anyone else, it means nothing. To me, it means he can't lose. Royal flush, probably. "You of all people understand the value of prime real estate, given you're a majority owner of this fine establishment and all. How do you feel about your investment here, by the way?"

Cohen bursts out in laughter. It's a reedy, sniffling sound. "You've got brass, I'll give you that. And you don't give up easily. Do you know how many conversations I've had just like this one?"

"Gabe." Farley's deep, grumbling voice fills my ear, pulling my attention away from the game. The bodyguard's face is grim. Then again, it's always grim.

"What is it?"

His square jaw tenses. "We had a visitor this morning."

My stomach tenses. "Our tails are finally wagging?" We've had federal agents on us since we left Phoenix, the morning after our plane went boom. Either they're amateurs, or they're not trying to hide the fact that they're monitoring us. Normally we wouldn't bat an eye at having shadows because we're not dumb enough to get caught, but after last night's unplanned massacre and emergency cleanup in our penthouse suite, the last thing we need are any of them sniffing around.

Our contacts within the department have confirmed that they've discovered the staged scene out in the desert, but there's no way they've identified the bodies yet. There isn't any proof that those men were in our penthouse suite last night—nothing that could produce a search warrant this quickly, anyway. The Perris came in through the service elevator and the security camera footage was wiped. Plus, Merrick's cleaner was top notch.

Farley shakes his head. "It's got nothing to do with them." The flash of apprehension in his eyes—almost like the giant wall of muscle is afraid to tell me—makes my insides twist. "It's Mercy."

TWO
MERCY

THE CARGO VAN hits another deep pothole. I grit my teeth against the harsh jolt that rattles my bones, but I don't dare release a sound.

I don't want my abductor to know I'm awake.

Our route has grown increasingly bumpy since I regained consciousness, maybe twenty minutes ago. I can't guess how long it's been since I opened the bathroom door in the hotel room and the man with the hideous scar across his face jabbed me in the neck with a needle. I blacked out and woke up lying on my side, still in my robe, with my arms bound behind my back, a sharp binding cutting into my wrists to keep them together.

Through the grimy back windows, the sun shines, hinting at daytime, but it was morning when he took me. We could be many hours from Vegas by now. Sweat clings to my skin, the stifling heat suffocating. I assume we're still in the desert, but the desert is a vast place.

And I'm in deep trouble.

Who is this guy, besides someone dangerous? And how did he get into a penthouse guarded by Gabriel's men? No one goes up that elevator unless they've been permitted, and I doubt Farley would give this creep a hall pass.

The service entrance. I'll bet that's how he made his way in. They smuggled three dead bodies out of there last night using the same route. This guy either knows the hotel well or pulled information from one of the staff. I cringe at the thought of how.

Does Gabriel know I've been kidnapped yet? Or will he be so tied up with trying to buy the Mage all day that he doesn't realize I'm gone until much later? Will he think I left? Woke up to a change of heart about him and this sordid life after last night's bloodbath?

And where are Moe and Michelle? They stayed behind with me in the penthouse. Do they know I'm gone? My kidnapper would have had to get through Moe to reach me, and Gabriel said the bodyguard was the best at what he does.

Not as good as this guy, apparently.

Did he kill Moe?

Is he going to kill me?

An odd, numb feeling courses through my veins.

The van takes a sharp right turn and then the road gets rougher, my shoulder and hip aching with each thump against the rigid metal floor. I get a moment's respite when we stop, just long enough for the driver to hop out. I strain to listen to a clank of metal and jangle of chain, and then he's climbing back in, slamming the door shut with a hollow thud. The van chugs forward once again.

"You can stop pretendin'. I know you're awake," a deep, croaky male voice calls out, bitter humor lacing his words.

I stiffen but don't respond.

"I'd put you at a buck twenty. A woman your size would have woken up about a half hour ago, even without the bumpy ride."

I swallow against my trepidation and feign a calm tone. "What'd you give me?"

"A sedative. Don't worry, you won't be drowsy for too much longer."

Because *that's* what I'm worried about. Though, having a clear head is better for thinking, and I need to think if I'm going to devise an escape plan. "Where are you taking me?"

"Somewhere no one will ever find you."

Does he believe that or is he just trying to scare me? If so, he has succeeded. A chill runs along my spine.

This couldn't have been a random kidnapping. It was too well planned. It must have something to do with Gabriel's uncle. He failed at blowing up the plane, so he's going a different route. But why take me? Why not wait in the room for the guys and end them?

Something doesn't add up.

Maybe it has nothing to do with the uncle. Maybe it's this cartel that Agent Lewis was talking about. Do they plan on holding me for ransom in exchange for territory? Do cartels do that sort of thing?

I know it's not the Perris, for obvious reasons.

What if this is something entirely different that Gabriel and his family are involved in, something I don't know about? How many enemies do the Eastons have, and why would someone go to all this trouble?

At least this guy is answering my questions, which means he might give me something of use. I force the tremor from my voice. "You're making a big mistake. Do you realize who I'm with?"

He snorts. "Why do you think you're in this mess? It's because of who you're with that you're here."

"And do you have any idea what he'll do to you when he finds you?" He doesn't sound at all concerned.

"Like I said, he ain't finding us. And you should be more worried 'bout yourself than what happens to me." The van comes to a skidding halt and the engine cuts off.

My panic swells as I listen to the man hop out of the driver's side. His shoes drag across gritty ground as he rounds the van. The back doors open with a yawning creak, and I cringe against the blinding sunlight that streams in. It's quickly forgotten though, when strong hands seize my ankles and drag me out. I scream and attempt to break free of his grip, but it's all in vain. I'll never fend him off, bound the way I am.

His fists lock around my biceps, and he hoists me to my feet. It allows me a better vantage point of my current situation. My eyes dart around, trying to gather as much information on my surroundings as I can, even in my foggy state of shock and my hunched position.

A single-wide mobile home sits ahead of me, its faded beige vinyl walls camouflaged in the sand. Maybe fifty feet away is a three-door metal garage with a green roof. Beyond it is nothing but flat desert, broken up by prickly vegetation and, in the far distance, low mountains.

Where are we? Nevada? Arizona? New Mexico?

A ten-foot-high chain-link fence capped with barbed wire circles the perimeter of what I assume is this man's compound. A battered green pickup truck sits off to one side, dusty and baking in the hot sun, its tires flat. Beside it, the top of a well juts out from the ground. A bucket sits next to it. To my right are solar panels, angled up to collect the sun's rays, along with multiple satellites to gather various signals. Along the side of the garage, in what might be the only slip of shade anywhere, is a line of plastic and metal drums, and several raised garden beds with tomatoes and green beans.

If I had to guess, I'd say this guy could survive out here on his own for months without ever making a run for supplies.

My gut tenses. How long will *I* survive out here?

"Get goin'." He shoves me forward and I stumble, the desert scalding beneath my bare feet. The tie on my robe has loosened, leaving the two sides hanging open and myself exposed. I'm too frightened to be embarrassed. Still, I'm thankful he's behind me as he goads me forward, up the metal steps and through the door that he reaches around me to open. He left it unlocked. I guess there was no need to secure it, what with our remote location and the barbed wire.

The air inside the trailer is stifling, the windows all sealed, the blinds closed to shut out the sun—or the outside world from the dark things happening inside. It's sparsely decorated and old, but tidy, and overwhelmingly clean. My nose furls at the overpowering scent of bleach.

"Move," he barks.

I stagger in the only direction I can—past the faded brown La-Z-Boy and television, through the kitchen that boasts ivory appliances and a 1950's style metal-and-melamine dinette set, along a narrow corridor of faux-wood-paneled walls and closet doors. Two doors are situated at the end. The one on the right has multiple locks on the outside.

I tense as he reaches around me to open the door to that room. With a slap against the light switch just inside, he herds me into a tiny space lit by one naked bulb and empty save for a bucket in a corner and a mattress lying on the floor. The only window in the room has been boarded up with a sheet of plywood, sealing it shut.

Not that I hadn't already guessed it, but this guy has prepared for me.

Fingers dig into my forearm behind my back, and I automatically squirm against his grip.

"Hold still or I'll cut you," he warns.

I wince as he tugs on my arms, but then the tension around my wrists loosens, the binding removed. I curl my arms around my body, pulling the sides of my robe closed as I shift away from him, into the corner.

Finally, I dare turn to face my captor for the first time since he took me.

My breath catches. It's not the scar running from his

temple to his jaw that makes me flinch, though that injury looks like it comes with a horrific tale. *Everything* about his face—from his hollowed cheeks to his sunken eyes to the thin, flat line of his mouth—is cold and hostile. He's wiry thin, his hair cropped short and graying at the temples. I'd put him in his late forties.

In his left grip is the knife he used to free my wrists—a long, curved blade that looks primed to gut a person. Those flinty gray eyes drag over the length of me, but the usual hunger I see lingering in men's gazes when they ogle me is absent. That almost scares me more.

He makes no move forward.

What does he plan on doing to me?

I swallow against my burgeoning fear and lift my chin, feigning confidence. "If you know who Gabriel Easton is, then you know how much money he has and how much he'd pay to get me back, unharmed." I hope that's all this is about. Gabriel's proven he's willing to pay to keep me around and happy. He's thrown obscene amounts of money at everyone—the guards at Fulcort to allow me access to my father; Justin DeHavilland, the lawyer who's convinced he can get my father's conviction overturned; even the drug rehab center where I work, to ensure they can afford to keep paying my salary. Surely, Gabriel will pay this guy whatever he wants.

One corner of the man's thin lips kicks up. "Probably not as much as his father is paying me to keep you here."

My eyes flash wide with surprise. This guy works for Vlad Easton? Gabriel's *father* is behind my kidnapping?

His dark chuckle fills the small, stuffy room. "Welcome to the family, darlin'. Haven't you realized just how fucked up they all are yet?"

"Why is Gabriel's father paying you to keep me here?"

"Because Vlad figured out what string to pull to get his son to do what he wants him to."

Realization hits me. Gabriel's father has been pressing him to take over the family's criminal enterprise, something both Gabriel and Caleb are desperate to get away from, if what Gabriel told me was true. "He won't do it."

"For your sake, you better hope his tune changes." The man lifts the blade in his hand and tests the curved hook at the end with the pad of his thumb. A bright spot of crimson blooms on his skin. He doesn't so much as flinch at the self-inflicted wound. "But for my sake, I hope you're right."

The grin he flashes turns my blood cold.

"Better get comfortable. You're in for some long days and nights." He leaves, pulling the door shut behind him.

I hold my breath and listen as several clicks sound, locking me in.

This is actually happening.

This is real.

What does he hope to do to me?

I scour every inch of my cell as hot tears stream down my cheeks, looking for an escape.

THREE
GABRIEL

"WHAT THE FUCK do you mean, *he got by you*?" My anger ricochets off the penthouse's looming ceilings. "We pay you assholes to *not* let guys like my father's hitman *get by you*!"

The bodyguards stand in a row, studying their shoes. They don't have answers for me, only excuses.

I turn to Moe, lying on a bedsheet on the marble floor, his face as pale as the white linen. "And it was *definitely* Bane who did this?"

"Yes," he pushes through gritted teeth, as the doctor willing to fix and not ask questions yanks a bullet out of his shoulder with his medical tweezers.

Blowing up our plane a few nights ago, now kidnapping my girlfriend right out of our hotel bedroom? Bane's been busy.

"He came in through the service elevator," Farley confirms.

"Well, no shit, what gave it away? *The dead body in front of it?*" Caleb snaps, throwing an arm toward where

Ross lies in a pool of blood, his throat slashed from ear to ear. He was livid when I dragged him away from the poker game prematurely and with a royal flush in his mitt, but thankfully his focus has shifted to what's important. "How long ago was Bane here?"

"An hour, tops. He must have slipped in just after the last check-in."

It was Michelle who answered Moe's phone in a panic when Farley called, screaming that Moe was unconscious and bleeding. Farley raced up to find Ross dead and Moe with a bullet in his shoulder, a used needle for whatever sedative Bane injected him with lying nearby.

"Is there *anyone* who doesn't know about that elevator? It's a goddamn parade entrance into this place!" An odd mixture of rage and fear claws at my chest, the latter being the most potent and raw. The most foreign to me. "And let me guess, the cameras didn't catch anything."

Farley's eyes flash to his guys before confirming my assumption with a head shake. "They're still down from last night."

From when we had to sneak three bodies out and cover up a triple murder. Not that having surveillance video would make any difference in this situation. Mercy is gone and we know who took her.

And I know why.

I pick up an empty tumbler from the counter and throw it across the room, hoping the simple act will release some of this overwhelming tension. The glass shatters against the far wall. None of Farley's men flinch—they know better than to react. The doctor's eyes flicker to me but he quickly shifts back to his patient.

"Calm down," Caleb warns.

It only stirs my ire. "Don't tell me to calm down! We were downstairs, playing a stupid game of cat and mouse with Cohen when we *should* have been up *here*." I should have come straight back to the penthouse after receiving that call from Stanley, knowing my father was up to something.

I should never have left her.

"Which is why Bane hit when he did. He knew where we were," Caleb counters evenly. "If he hadn't taken her this morning, he would have got to her some other way."

He's right, but that doesn't make me feel better. Was Bane sitting in the lobby, watching? He couldn't have been. It's impossible to miss that face. "*You know* what that psychopath is capable of." The guy takes the task of dragging answers out of people too literally. My gut clenches at the thought of his sadistic hands on Mercy's body.

But it's guilt that is quickly taking root, readying to fester. Mercy is in danger because of me. Because I'm a selfish prick who forced an innocent woman into our blood-drenched life and plied her with money and charm and promises of a better life. I should have known there was only one way this was ever going to go —badly, for her. I should have known, when our father started asking about the inmate I've been paying to protect—Mercy's father—that he'd find a way to use her, that she'd be his ticket to getting me to do anything he wants.

Caleb's jaw tenses. He shifts his attention to the bleeding bodyguard on the floor. "Doc?"

The stout man's fingers move quickly with needle and thread. "Flesh wound. A deep one, but he should be fine with rest. Nothing vital was hit."

"Lucky son of a bitch," one of the idiot guards murmurs.

"It has nothing to do with luck. Moe's gonna be fine because Bane allowed it," I hiss, pacing around the vast common room. They have no clue who they're dealing with. Hell, we probably don't know everything about who we're dealing with. Bane—as he goes by—has revealed little over the years to my father. We dug up a few details from his time in the military, namely that he was dishonorably discharged for using "questionable" tactics to interrogate the enemy about their operations, a dirty secret that was buried to avoid sullying senior officers who knew but looked the other way. The guy was trained to hunt and to survive. He can slip through any net or trap. Drop him in a deadly jungle with no supplies and when you go back to pick him up in a month, he'll be waiting for you, ten pounds heavier and no worse for wear.

I stab my index finger toward Moe. "You think he missed? You think he didn't put that bullet *exactly* where he wanted it to go?" Avoiding the artery so Moe didn't bleed out before he woke up from whatever Bane pumped into his vein. Bane doesn't miss, he doesn't make mistakes. He didn't need to shoot Moe to incapacitate him, he *chose* to. But he wanted Moe alive to relay a message—that Vlad Easton was here, that he can reach us from the depths of his Fulcort prison cell, whenever he wants. Just like it wasn't a mistake that Bane's face was caught on surveillance footage at the explosion. Dad knew we'd use our resources to tap into whatever the feds uncover. He wanted us to figure out who was behind that.

And now my father has me right where he wants me —willing to do *anything* to get Mercy back, including cementing myself in the Easton family drug empire that I've been so desperate to wash my hands of.

What were his instructions to Bane? Has he given him a free pass to hurt her if I don't comply? From what I've heard, Bane isn't the type to find pleasure in a woman's body—whether by forcing himself or with a willing participant—but that's a small blessing considering the kinds of things he *does* take pleasure in.

Caleb sighs and turns his attention to Michelle, perched on a barstool, her hands stained with Moe's blood, a dazed look in her big blue eyes. Farley found her next to Moe, pressing a towel against his wound to stop the bleeding. Thank God she wasn't foolish enough to call the hotel line for help. That would have made the situation a thousand times worse. "You didn't see or hear anything?"

She shakes her head. "Just Moe's phone ringing for a long time. That's why I came out of my room. I must have been in the shower when that guy was here. I didn't hear any gunshot," she whispers hoarsely, her damp hair proof of her claim.

"So Bane *let* you live too, then."

The way she shrinks away from my brother's cold gaze, no one would ever guess they were happily swapping bodily fluids less than twenty-four hours ago. Of everyone in this room, Mercy's best friend might have had the roughest few days, what with the feds using fraud charges against her father to manipulate her into informing on us while on this trip. Thankfully, we discovered it before she was able to give them anything useful, and now that Caleb has scared her into silence over the litany of dead bodies she witnessed last night, she's the least of our worries. She's just another casualty of being too close to the Eastons. I *almost* feel sorry for her.

But right now, I don't give a fuck about her or a hemorrhaging Moe or anyone else. All I care about is finding Mercy.

"Does he actually think he'll get what he wants, pulling this shit?" Caleb slips a cigarette into his mouth and lights it.

I haven't enlightened him about Stanley's earlier phone call and I can't, yet. If my brother finds out our father was behind the plane blowing up, that Finn and Felix are dead because of our father's little power game, he'll be hiring an inmate to snap the old man's neck before I can get a clue as to Mercy's whereabouts.

"I'm going to Fulcort," I announce. There's no way to deal with our father other than face-to-face.

"You're playing right into him, giving him what he wants—"

"What other choice do I have?" I bellow.

Caleb raises his hands in a sign of surrender. "Right. Of course, bro. Do what you gotta do. I get it."

He doesn't though. He doesn't have the first damn clue.

He's never been in love.

When I admitted that to her last night, it came as a surprise, as much to me as I assume to her. I've never said those words to anyone; I sure as hell have never felt them. But I know that's what this is, without a doubt, because I can't think past this reality that she's gone and I don't want to keep breathing unless I have her back.

Smoke permeates the air as Caleb puffs on his cigarette and scans the situation in our penthouse. "As much as I'd love to visit Daddy-O *again*, I'll stay here and play like all is copacetic for our admirers. After last night, we can't both take off abruptly. It'll raise flags."

He's right about that, too. "Farley will come with me. The rest of them stay here."

Farley's head bobs once in confirmation. A throat clears somewhere in the room. We're not used to having an audience as we work through our family issues, but the team of bodyguards, the doctor, Michelle…, none of them matter.

"Keep people the fuck out of here," I warn.

"That's a given at the moment, I'd say, bro?" Caleb gaze drifts over the penthouse, over the bloody towels and ashen-faced Moe, then toward the hall that leads to where Ross bled out.

"Shouldn't we call the police?" Michelle's voice is shaky and small, so unlike her.

Caleb snorts. "For what?"

She falters, taken aback. "I mean… Mercy's been kidnapped. They'll help us find her."

"Oh, you sweet girl. Still so naïve." He tsks. "You think they have the first damn clue where to look for her? We have a better shot of finding her on our own."

"I just thought…."

"The last thing we need is anyone snooping around in here, including your new best friend, Agent Lewis, downstairs. You think she cares what happens to Mercy? Only if it helps her case." Caleb slips Michelle's phone out of his pocket, the one he confiscated last night, and waves it in the air. "And if *she* gets involved, I promise you'll *never* see Mercy alive again. We all know you stabbed her in the back, but is that what you want?"

Michelle answers him with a vehement headshake, her eyes watering.

"Well then, don't get any ideas. You just keep playing along like life's one big happy party then, while Gabe and I deal with this family matter." With a heavy sigh, he slides his own phone out and mutters, "Merrick's cleaner is quickly depleting my gambling cash."

I don't care if we don't have two coins to rub together, if it means finding Mercy. "Keep me updated." I charge for the elevator, not waiting to confirm that Farley is following.

"Didn't expect to see you back here again so soon," Donny drawls, his keys jangling against his side with each step as he leads me along the narrow, dank corridor and into an older, rarely used section of the prison.

"Yeah, me neither," I grumble. My visits are growing more frequent rather than less, the exact opposite of what I want. Then again, it serves as an icy cold shower to my reality. If I give my father everything he wants, I could end up behind these bars with him.

I could end up as hateful and twisted as he is.

"You know, these types of visits are *a lot* easier to arrange after hours."

"I don't give a shit what's easy," I snap, my mood steeped in bitterness after spending the four-hour drive here playing all kinds of Saw-like horror flick scenarios about what Bane could be doing to Mercy's flawless body in my imagination.

I pay to have the Fulcort guard in my pocket when it's needed for *me*, not when it's convenient for him. And I pay him a truck's worth. Or a fully loaded GTO's worth, to be more accurate. All of these damn guards have been well compensated several times over since Vlad Easton climbed into his orange jumpsuit. Enough that they shouldn't be uttering a word of complaint.

"Any news on Chops's next match?" Donny asks, now with a touch of hesitation.

"No." The last thing I care about is providing these degenerates their prison fight entertainment. Not unless my father is Chops's opponent, and I'll want a front row seat for that.

Donny glances over his shoulder at me but doesn't say anything more—wise choice. If he couldn't guess by my stony face when I arrived that I'm not doing idle chatter today, he's figured it out by now.

The infamous Vlad Easton is waiting for me in the small room, leaning back in his chair, his legs sprawled, his bloated belly pressing against the edge of the table. A smug look is plastered across his pockmarked face as he watches me. He's wearing bruises from the little tussle he and Caleb got into the last time we visited, which makes sense seeing as Caleb's eye is still a mottled blueish purple.

"I got you ten minutes. Fifteen minutes, tops, before the supe starts—"

"I'll take as long as I need." I cut off Donny's warning and dismiss him from my attention, marching toward the table in the center of the room, willing my fists to unclench as I take in the hateful bastard who gave me life.

The outer door clicks quietly behind me, leaving Dad and me locked in a staring contest for three beats.

"Another private visit and so soon. I *am* loved by my children after all," he says after a moment.

He knows why I'm here, and all I want to do is reach across the table and choke the answer out of him. At the same time, I can't ignore that twinge of hurt—of betrayal—that pricks my chest. I always knew our father was capable of being cruel, but I guess I was dumb enough to convince myself he wouldn't do something as vicious as this to me.

I give a cursory glance at the cameras to make sure the lights are off and then I pull out the chair opposite my father and slide into it. "Where is she, you sick son of a bitch."

A glimmer of satisfaction flashes in his eyes. "Finally, I see some of my own fire in you. I always knew Caleb had it. I was beginning to worry about you."

"You're about to see more than fire if you don't cough up a location." My tone is icier than I've ever dared use with him.

He drags his thumb across his bottom lip in thought. "When I heard that a woman managed to tie a leash to my baby boy, I didn't believe it at first. The only thing more shocking would be to see Caleb settling down."

"Your source is shit. There's no leash on me. She's just a good lay," I lie.

"You could have bought fifty good lays for what you must be spending on her father's legal fees." Dad smirks. "Nothing stays quiet in these walls. Haven't you figured that out yet?"

And here I was, worrying about Camillo or Miles finding out about Mercy.

I'll bet that gossip Parker has been spilling his guts about who's checking in to see Duncan. I'll be paying the guard a visit to his house after this is all over and making sure his tongue never wags again.

"How did the meeting with the Perris go?"

So, we're going to dance a little before he fesses up to his crimes. "Fan-fucking-tastic."

"Then why were their dismembered and burned bodies discovered outside of Las Vegas early this morning?" His steady eyes dissect me.

I grit my molars to keep from cursing. The feds know what they've found—the SUV left at the scene was registered to Miles Perri—but the news hasn't broken yet, which means that even within these thick concrete walls, basically waiting for his bloated, worn body to give out on him, Vlad still has his fingers in every pot and people willing to feed him whatever he wants. I'd say I don't know how he maintains such power, but I do. Money and fear—two formidable tools in his belt. The latter, he wields especially well. He has decades of experience.

"I don't know what to tell you, except we met with the Perris, we discussed the arrangement, they agreed, and then they left."

He smooths a palm over his stomach. "Did you practice that bullshit answer on the drive over here?"

"It's not bullshit." It's just not the entire truth. They *did* leave.

Buried in laundry hampers.

Not breathing.

His laughter is deep, grating. "I know my sons too well, and this stinks of your brother's temper. I expected as much, putting him in a room with Miles Perri." The smile Dad flashes is nothing short of proud. "Glad to see Caleb hasn't disappointed me in that regard."

What is he saying? That he *expected* Caleb to go all *Wild Wild West* and gun down the Perris? "Then why the fuck did you make us meet with them!"

"Because either you'd form an alliance and deal with Navarro together, or Caleb would remove the Perris from the equation and open up their territory," he barks.

"Either scenario benefits us and that is all I care about. That my family is taken care of."

I shake my head. He only cares about his family so long as it's a possession to him, something he can claim and control. But it's not surprising that the old man's been scheming all along. "And what about what you had Bane do to our plane? How does blowing up your two sons benefit *us*?"

His chapped lips twist. "That was a lesson. An important one that it was time you two learned."

"A *lesson*?" At least he's not trying to deny it. But a lesson is teaching your son how to toss a ball or ride a bike, or maybe letting them spend the night in the slammer after they've gotten drunk and stirred up trouble with the local authorities. "He killed four innocent people!"

"Don't be naïve. No one's truly innocent in this world." He waves away my words. "And you fools are still too busy chasing pussy to pay attention to the threats around you. See how easy it was? Navarro can get to you like that." He snaps his fingers in the air. "It's time for that to change, if you're going to survive in this business."

That's the thing: I don't want to survive in this business. I want nothing to do with it. Both of us want out. But it doesn't matter to Vlad. It's his way, or his way by force. And I'm quickly losing track of the reason for my visit, the *only* thing I care about. I lean forward. "Where did Bane take Mercy?"

"She's safe for the moment," he answers cryptically.

Just being in a room with Bane is hazardous to

anyone's health. "He killed one of my bodyguards. Injured another."

"You should hire better bodyguards."

I slam my fist against the cold metal table surface. My patience, already balancing on the edge of a cliff when I stepped into this room, has officially evaporated. "Give her back to me now!" Not that Mercy is a possession but….

She's mine.

And nothing will be right in my life until she's in my arms again.

Anger burns in my father's eyes. His tolerance for this game is waning, too, it would seem. "She's somewhere no one will find her unless *I* allow it."

I force myself to take a deep, calming breath. "And what? You thought that if you kidnapped Mercy, I'd become your puppet? You say jump and I say how high?" Not that it hasn't been the way things have worked up until now, but I've always done it reluctantly, while looking for a way to avoid it altogether.

"Listen to me, you little shit. I didn't spend a lifetime of risking my freedom and ending up in *here*, only to rot while watching my two idiot sons piss away all that I've accomplished. It's time you two grow up and step into the roles that I've carved out for you."

"I didn't ask for whatever you've been carving for me."

"No, you've just happily reaped the harvest of it, haven't you," he sneers. "I've spent years taking care of you. Now you will take care of me while I'm stuck in here. That's your responsibility. I've asked nicely to no avail. You've left me with no other choice, Gabriel."

That simmering rage inside me begins to bubble. "So, blowing up our plane and abducting my girlfriend is on us, is it? This is all our fault? Is that what you're trying to tell me?" Typical narcissistic answer.

His eyes narrow. "It's certainly insurance so that my dear loving sons guarantee my remaining *years* in this shithole are palatable." I can't help but note the emphasis on years. It's as if he caught wind to what we've been planning with Vince and Merrick Perri. Maybe he has. Maybe that's what all this is about, in which case I don't have a right to be angry. "And now you'll take your rightful spot at the head of the family. You and Caleb both. Your brother may have the temperament to survive this world, but you're the level-headed one. The one who will hold everything together."

Dad is nothing if not persistent, I'll give him that. Then again, what else does the guy have to hold onto, sitting in his little concrete cell? He needs the Easton name thriving on the outside, or the ring of protection he's cocooned himself in on the inside will vanish and he'll just be another sad old criminal in a cage, only with too many enemies to count. "What about Peter? I think he'll have something to say about us claiming that title. Everyone does what he says." It's always been Vlad and Peter Easton at the helm, and since Dad was locked up —thanks to Peter's betrayal—Uncle Peter has managed the big decisions. All of our cousins and business associates answer to him, and he's made it clear that he wants us out of the way.

"He is no longer an issue for us. Neither are those idiots he calls sons." Dad's flat, cold gaze says it all.

Bane must have found them. Busy hitman indeed. Has he already killed them? Dad seems unbothered by the fact that his brother and nephews are dead—or soon to be—by his order. But I don't give a shit about my uncle or my cousins. Peter signed his death certificate the day he decided to betray his brother for his own gain. All I care about is seeing Mercy again, alive and safe, and I know my father won't budge.

"Tell Bane to stay the hell away from her. You got that?" I warn.

"You two start behaving and I'll have no reason to tell him otherwise." Dad smirks. "But from what I've heard around here, even that sick son of a bitch might feel his little dick twitch at the sight of her—"

The metal chair legs scrape against the concrete floor as I bolt out of my chair and reach across the table. I grab my father by the collar of his prison-issue uniform and haul him forward, until our faces our inches apart. "If he lays a single finger on her," I force through gritted teeth, "so help me God, I will end you—"

"Enough of this!" Dad shoves me away with force. He takes a moment to adjust his top button. "You're wasting time, and we have important things to discuss."

Of course. It's always about the business. My father is an unmovable ten-tonne boulder. Threats have never swayed him.

I check the door and see Donny peeking through the tiny window. He must have heard the commotion. After the last visit and my sour mood, I'll bet he's worried he'll have a dead body to explain. I pick my chair off the floor and take my seat again. "And what exactly do we have to discuss, *father*?"

He arranges his hands in a tent on the table in front of him. "Harriet's escorts have informed me that they are no longer interested in their paid position."

God damn Harriet. *Call it what it is*, I want to scream. *Your cocaine and heroin empire!* He's so used to using his stupid code names, it's engrained in him.

"You're surprised by this?" Puff's guys keep getting massacred by the cartel for muling drugs for us. "So pay them more."

"They just cost us a significant sum when they let Navarro burn our product. Why would I pay them *more* when they haven't done their job? If anything, they should compensate us."

"Yeah, good luck with that." There's no way Puff's crew can scrape together that kind of cash. We're talking about millions. Plus, they've probably heard what happened to the Mamba who was interrogated by the cartel for intel. His motorcycle club found him with his manhood jammed in his mouth like a festive pig biting an apple. "I guess Puff doesn't feel that the risk of mutilation and dismemberment is worth being in business with us anymore." Can't say I blame him.

"And that is where you come in. I need you to convince him that it is in his best interest to continue with our arrangement," he says slowly, clearly. "Send a message. Remind him that he has loved ones. Take away their freedom until he comes to his senses."

He wants me to threaten Puff. Or, more aptly, Puff's family, who's on the outside while he sits in these walls along with my father, surrounded by his own ring of protection. Virtually untouchable.

Caleb and I have stepped in from time to time to settle questions about who's in charge when it comes to gangsters and other lowlifes, but we've always drawn the line at innocents. Women and children are off-limits.

But now my father has my balls in an iron vice, primed to squeeze, and we both know it.

"Is that all…." I feign a dull tone, meanwhile my insides are twisting.

"No, but that's a start."

It's never just one thing with him. "And what else are we being tasked to do?"

"There's a shipment coming from Eduardo next week. Ivan will handle it, but he has *your* number now instead of Peter's."

"Fine. Whatever." Eduardo has been running the cartel in Sinaloa for years. He's a mean fucker, but he and Dad have always gotten along well. And Ivan is basically my father's and Uncle Peter's righthand man. He's the guy dad trusted most after Uncle Peter. He's been managing all the cocaine supply runs since before Dad went to prison.

It's a relatively smooth operation. Aside from fielding a phone call from Ivan to confirm it's done, I don't have to do anything except remind Ivan who he works for so he doesn't get any ideas, now that Peter, Vic, and Alexei are gone for good. "Are we done then?"

Dad studies his chewed fingernails. "I heard there were only three Perris found this morning. Why not five?"

I shrug. I can't explain that without incriminating myself. I won't try.

"They need to be dealt with."

Jesus. Now he's ordering us to kill Vince and Merrick? "Why?"

"Because your brother has created an opportunity for us, one I don't want to waste. It'll be cleaner for us to take over the Perri territory if there aren't two of them alive to challenge us, and we need to do it now, before Navarro makes his move."

The last thing Merrick and Vince care to do is take on Vlad Easton *or* Navarro for their stake in the Perri drug business, but my father doesn't know that, and *I'm* not supposed to know that. "Navarro's already making his move for that territory."

"He'll back down."

"Why would he do that? So far he's been handing us our asses." Slaughtering our distribution chain and burning our product in a masterful "fuck you." "Now you want to take on *more* territory that he wants, with less people in our corner to defend us?" I snort. "You've officially lost your damn mind."

"He *will* back down, when he learns that the Easton family is not to be trifled with." A small smirk touches his lips.

My eyes narrow with suspicion. "What have you set in motion?"

"A lesson. You don't need the details."

Shit. I know what his lessons look like, firsthand. "So, you're starting an all-out war with Navarro's cartel that we'll have to clean up," I say flatly. Tossing a lit match onto a pile of tinder.

"No, I'm going to show him that our reach can be just as long and punishing."

A knock sounds on the door. Donny is eyeing me through the window, a pained expression plastered across his face. If he has the guts to pressure me like this, it means this conversation has to end now before this channel is permanently blocked.

"Those two Perris? They're a problem. Deal with them." Dad's bushy eyebrows arch in meaning.

I can't begin to wrap my head around these requests —murder, abduction, maybe more murder—and whether I'll comply. It's a good thing I have a long drive back to Vegas to consider my options. If I'm foolish enough to believe I have any. But he still hasn't given me an answer. "Where is she?"

He hesitates on his response, watching me a moment. "I told you. She's safe. Probably safer now than she is when she's with you. Definitely safer than she would be in Navarro's hands."

My molars grind against each other.

"Consider it a favor that I'm doing for you, son. You need to focus on your priorities. She'll stay safe while you learn how to run the business."

I fight the urge to reach across the table and choke

the answer out of him. I'd never get it. He'd die with a smile on his lips and a promise on his tongue, that Mercy will suffer extra for my betrayal. "I expect a phone call within the hour with her on the other line." I need to at least hear her voice, to tell her I'm sorry.

I need to hear her tell me that she doesn't hate me.

That she still loves me.

Dad snorts. "Bane doesn't work like—"

"Within the hour!" My shout ricochets off the walls as I storm out.

FOUR
MERCY

Forty-two.

That's how many nails my captor drove through the sheet of plywood to secure it to the window, shutting the world out. Ten would have sufficed. Regardless, I don't have a hope in hell of prying it off, a reality I accepted hours ago, after pacing the perimeter of this tiny bedroom until the stifling air exhausted me. After making sure there weren't any hidden cameras, I shed my robe, the hefty terry cloth smothering in this intolerable heat.

It was around that same time that I heard the woman's scream for the first time.

The frightened sound came from somewhere outside of the trailer—the garage, probably.

She sounded older and her cries were interspersed with pleading. There were so many "please don'ts" and "we'll give you anythings." I don't know who "we" is or what she was begging our captor not to do. Knowing that I'm not the only one trapped in this desert compound brought me a twisted comfort, but I haven't heard her again in some time. *That* doesn't bring me *any* comfort.

I assume she's stuck here on Vlad Easton's orders. I wonder what she did to earn his ire?

All *I* did was fall in love with his son.

With a deep breath to stifle my panic, my thoughts drift to Gabriel. He *must* know by now that I've been taken, and I'm sure he's beyond livid. But has he figured out that it's his own father directing this psychopath?

He'll find me and get me out of here. I know he will. For all Gabriel's faults—and he has many—he has always protected me in his own way. Will he get the police involved though? No, not likely and especially not after what happened in the penthouse last night.

But he's probably already running around with his team of bodyguards, on the phone with his P.I, breaking all kinds of laws and throwing money at people for information. Someone *must* have seen something. Me, carried into the van. Cameras that caught the plates. *Anything.*

Gabriel will save me. I just need to be patient.

I check the plastic water bottle in my grip. The amount left in it hasn't changed—a mouthful. It was full when he locked me in here and I've been savoring it over the hours. I'm not eager to use the bucket in the corner—presumably the restroom. Also, I have no idea how long it'll be before I get another. This guy doesn't seem like the type to be too concerned about keeping me hydrated.

An ear-piercing shriek slices through the silence.

My heart begins to race. It's that woman again, only it's a different sound than the last round of screams, laced less with fear and more with horror.

I hold my breath and listen for some clue about who she is, and why she's trapped here, too.

Another shriek punctures the desert's quiet soon after, this one more desperate.

I jolt at the blast of a gunshot and my blood turns cold at the deathly silence that follows.

Did he just kill her?

Am I next in line?

Will I be screaming and begging for my life soon, too?

Something tells me pleading with this guy would be useless.

I slip my robe back on and pull it tight around my body for comfort as terror threatens to overwhelm me. And I focus on positive thoughts: that Gabriel will find me.

He'll save me.

I can't say how much time passes before I hear heels dragging across sand, shortly before boots climb the metal steps. My pulse races in my ears as the mobile door creaks open. "Gimme a minute. I was in the middle of the other job when you called," my kidnapper says, his voice gruff and annoyed. "Yeah, yeah… you know I don't normally cater to this shit." He's talking to someone on the phone. Cupboard doors slam. "Okay, shoot…. Yup. As soon as I hang up with you." A heavy sigh and curse follow, and then footfalls approach slowly along the hallway.

I scramble to stand and tie my robe tight around me, my bladder threatening to loosen from my building nerves. I dart to the far corner.

Is this where he drags me out to his shed to show me his gun?

I'll fight him, if I must.

A series of latches and locks flip and turn and then the door to my room swings open and the man steps through the doorway. My knees buckle at the sight of the beige butcher's apron covering his torso, drenched in fresh blood.

He has an old flip phone pressed to his ear. "You got ten seconds," he barks, before closing the distance and holding it out toward me.

I swallow my terror. "Who is it—"

"Talk to him or don't, I don't give a shit, but stop wasting my time!"

There's only one *him* it could be. I snatch the phone from the man's grip. "Hello?"

"Mercy. Thank God." Gabriel's raspy voice fills my ear. "Are you okay?"

Hot tears stream down my cheeks, unbidden. "I don't know?" I'm being held captive by a man wearing an apron covered in what I assume is human blood. I'm *far* from okay. But, as terrified as I am, a small bloom of hope swells in my chest. Gabriel has already tracked me down. I'm closer to getting out of here than I was two minutes ago.

"Has Bane hurt you in *any* way?"

So that's his name. Gabriel knows this guy. Then he must also have figured out that his father is behind this. I swallow and shake my head, then remember that he can't see me. "No."

"Okay, that's…." His heavy sigh screams of relief. "Don't be scared. He's not going to lay a finger on you. I promise."

The man—Bane—eyes me like a coiled cobra, looking ready to strike. I don't share Gabriel's confidence. "Please get me out of here," I plead.

"I swear, babe, as soon as I can figure out where you are, I'm coming to get you, and no one will *ever* do this to us again." That last part he says through gritted teeth. He's furious. Good. But there's also something else lingering there in his voice, an emotion I've never sensed from Gabriel before.

Fear.

He's afraid.

And that terrifies me.

"We're somewhere in the desert—"

Bane snatches the phone from my grasp, spearing me with a warning glare before pressing it to his ear. As if I could tell Gabriel anything useful to tracking me down. "You wanted proof of life and you got it," he barks. "Now I got things to finish up for your old man." He scowls at the wall. I can't hear what Gabriel is saying but the deep, angry hum of his voice carrying through the receiver is surely laced with harsh threats. "What do you think I am, a babysitter? You're in no position to be ordering me around." He laughs. "I work for your father, not you. And *no one* tells me what to do. She'll stay unharmed as long as she isn't a pain in my ass." He spears me with a glare. "And you'll hear from her again when I feel like it. Maybe I won't feel like it. Eat shit." He jabs the end call button with his thumb in a poor replacement for slamming a receiver down. "Call him every hour on the hour so he can talk to you," he mutters under his breath. "Who the hell does he think he is."

Is that what Gabriel demanded? It brings me an unexpected shroud of comfort, but it's quickly consumed by the reality that Gabriel is legitimately afraid for me.

"These Eastons and all their fucking requirements. I've about had enough of them."

I swallow my trepidation and try to seize an opportunity. "Sounds like you should make a deal with Gabriel then. You know he'll pay you to let me go. *A lot.* More than what his father is paying you to keep me." Would he?

"That's the problem with your generation. No loyalty. You'll flip on a dime." Bane shakes his head. "I'll say one thing though, Vlad was right, that guy sure is riled up about you. Don't know what's so special...." His narrow eyes drag over my robe, down to my bare ankles, where they stall a moment.

I shrink back, afraid where those thoughts are veering. I don't see any hint of lust burning in those dark eyes, but I don't see much of *anything*, which is far more alarming.

Thankfully his gaze shifts, wandering around my room, stalling on the empty water bottle. He purses his lips. "Don't get any ideas," he warns and marches out.

Leaving the door wide open.

In my mind, I'm sprinting down the narrow hall, shoving his wiry frame aside and escaping. But my body is frozen in place, my gut telling me that plan won't end as I'm picturing it. Besides, wandering in the vast desert in bare feet and a terry-cloth robe—in August—would be a guaranteed death sentence.

He returns ten seconds later, a small brown leather suitcase clattering behind him. In his other hand is a fresh bottle of water. He tosses them both to the floor. "Here."

I eye the Louis Vitton branding on the suitcase. "Whose is it?" Someone with money, clearly.

"Don't matter. She won't be needing any of it anymore."

He must be talking about the woman who just finished screaming into the end of a gun barrel. Is that her blood that Bane's wearing? It must be.

Because if it's not hers, then who else has he murdered today?

With a thin, vicious smile, he leaves, this time pulling the door shut behind him. The multitude of latches click in place.

FIVE
GABRIEL

I'VE ALWAYS preferred arriving in Sin City at night, its lure of flashy signs and bright lights an intoxicating start to any visit. Tonight though, as Farley pulls into the Mage's laneway after the arduous trip to and from Fulcort, all I can think about is the fear that drenched Mercy's voice.

"Fucking *find her*!" I hiss, squeezing my phone to try and release some of this never-ending tension that's gripped me since Mercy was kidnapped.

"I'm *trying*, Gabe! I told you, it isn't that easy!" Stanley says. "I don't know which burner Vlad's using to contact him but it ain't any that you gave him, and Bane must be using an encryption on his end to stop a trace. I can't find any record of where he's been living. He's a ghost, past his military record."

I've already called the P.I. a dozen times today, hounding him to break every law and pay every shady fuck he knows whatever they want in order to track down this lair where Bane's holding her. If I had to guess, it's remote and well fortified. I doubt our father knows where it is. But *someone* must. That it's in the desert is disconcerting. That's a lot of ground to cover.

I know Stanley's trying and he's one of the best at what he does, but even that isn't good enough right now.

My phone rang sixty-seven minutes after I passed through Fulcort's gates, seven minutes after the one-hour deadline I gave my father, as I was toiling with the idea of calling Donny and arranging for Chops to pay a special late-night visit to my father's cell. Dad made me wait just long enough to reinforce who's in control here, and it sure as hell ain't me.

The call with her was so quick, I had no time to think, to say what I wanted to say. She was there and then she was gone, and I was left dealing with that prick, spewing threats that I knew wouldn't persuade him in the least.

Please get me out of here.

Hearing her plead for me to rescue her nearly broke me. My father might as well be holding my heart at knifepoint. He's not going to give Bane the release order any time soon, not when he can force me to do his bidding, not when taking Mercy from me ensures he'll stay cozy and warm in his cell. I'm his puppet now. I can't escape his life plan for me anymore, not as long as he holds what I care about most in this world.

Well played, father.

The only way out of this mess is to find Mercy. We find her, and Vlad Easton is going to learn a lesson of his own.

A final lesson, one I'll happily deliver myself without an ounce of guilt tied to it.

He wanted to see my angry side? Well, he's damn well got it now.

"What can I do to help you find that son of a bitch?" I ask.

"Get me the burner Vlad's been calling Bane on, for starters. Do that, and I might be able to track down his location."

Easier said than done. I could get one of the guards to toss his cell—something we pay weekly to ensure *never* happens—but Dad's a master at playing both offensive and defensive. Who knows what fail-safes he has set up in the likelihood that he anticipates that? Bane could move Mercy.

He could torture her.

He could kill her.

"Keep looking for them." I end the call as Farley rolls up to the hotel valet. The staff rushes forward but he doesn't unlock the door for them yet.

"You wanna go in through the garage and take the service elevator up instead? Avoid people? I can park us," he offers.

"Why not? Everyone else and their damn mother is using that elevator to get in," I mutter. But no, that's not how we operate and, with that agent and her pals watching.... "Nah. Status quo is the way to go." Strolling into the lobby like I don't have a care in the world.

And yet I can't seem to will my body to move, because pretending that everything is fine when rage and panic are coursing through my veins at a steady thrum is impossible.

He hesitates. "We're gonna find her, Gabe."

"You better fucking hope so." I level him with a look that says the fault for Mercy being kidnapped sits squarely on his shoulders, when I know it's not Farley's fault that this happened, or Moe's or even my father's—though he is the catalyst.

I've done this to Mercy. Dragging her into my life has put her in a world of danger that I can't get her out of.

And if anything happens to her….

I grit my teeth against the hollow ache in my chest and slide on a mask of calm. "Let's go." It's time I enlightened my brother on exactly how far down this dark hole my father has hurled us.

Our elevator doors part to the sound of blaring music. I pause a moment to take in the horde of people milling around the penthouse. A few, I recognize. Most, I'm sure I've never seen before in my life. None of them should be here, but Caleb only knows how to do Vegas one way, and this is it. When Farley's detail at the bottom of the elevator informed us of our guests, I wasn't entirely surprised.

I can only assume Ross's body has long since been cleaned up. Caleb is reckless but he's no idiot.

I clench my jaw to keep my temper at bay—the Easton boys always like a good party after all—and shift past a group of women, brushing aside the clawed hand that reaches for me without acknowledging its owner. Maybe I know some of them—been inside a few—but none of them matter. No one matters anymore but Mercy.

"Where is he?" I scan the terrace beyond the wall of glass, but I don't see Caleb amongst the small crowd.

"My guess would be in there." Farley nods toward the games room. The doors are cracked open, the sound of female laughter carrying out.

"You've gotta be fucking kidding me." I charge in. Sure enough, the location for a triple homicide only twenty-four hours ago is now the host of a lively game of strip poker between Caleb, Merrick, Vincent, and four women who probably haven't seen their twentieth birthday and are sorely losing.

The air reeks of booze and perfume and sin.

"Hey, bro!" Caleb hollers, as if nothing's the matter. "You made good time! You gonna join the next round?" He's lost nothing more than the cufflinks off his shirt, though the material is rumpled, the buttons misaligned as if hastily fastened. Merrick and Vince are similarly dressed—fully, but dishevelled. Merrick, at least, grips his card hand, seemingly intent on the game, but Vince isn't intent on anything but the woman perched on his lap, wearing only her heels.

"Am I gonna join the next round?" I echo my brother's question, my voice unnaturally calm. Caleb's eyes are glossy and the table's surface in front of him is coated in white powder, which tells me what he's been up to all afternoon. That and the countless torn condom wrappers crumpled on the black marble floor, and his belt and shoes strewn near the leather couches. This game is just another act in the night, likely with fresh women after he finished with the last ones.

This is just Caleb being Caleb, I remind myself, as I reach down to untangle the skimpy red lace thong that somehow looped over my shoe.

But, while I've had to contend with our father and his laundry list of murder and abduction requests, and Mercy is trapped in the desert with a psychopath who could write a book on the art of torture, Caleb's been getting high and sticking his dick in wherever he can find room.

That's the last thing I need him to be doing right now.

"Everyone, get the fuck out now!" One look at Farley, who knows better than to stall, and he's moving swiftly out the door. In seconds, the music cuts off and disgruntled voices buzz as people are ushered out.

But in this room, no one moves.

"Did you not hear me! *Now*!" I'm seconds from pulling out my gun for a little show and scare to get them moving.

"Sorry, ladies. Gabe's got his panties in a bunch tonight." Caleb throws his cards to the table in an exaggerated display of annoyance. "That's two times today you've made me toss a royal flush."

The women climb out of their seats languidly, wearing pouts as they collect the few articles of clothing they arrived in before sashaying past me, offering everything from wariness to open disdain, as if I dared ruin their night.

The Perris don't even feign to wonder if I mean them, too. They stay settled like the partners in crime that they are.

My hand twitches at my side, the Glock tucked into my pants weighty, the guilt on my conscience more so. What would they say if they knew my father ordered them dead? Despite everything, I like these two. They're a lot like us, surviving in a world they were forced into and a path they're trying to break free of.

But if it's a choice between them and Mercy, I'll end them with a pull of my trigger, no questions asked.

First though, I need to fully consider my options and to do that, I need to have a sober conversation with my brother, who's currently coked out. "Are you a fucking idiot?" I stare at Caleb before pointedly looking around the room. I shouldn't have to elaborate.

"Actually, I'm pretty damn smart, if I do say so myself." He reaches for his rocks glass and takes a big swig. It's whiskey tonight instead of his usual vodka. "No one's gonna wonder why the room is pristinely clean, almost like a professional was in here."

He means a forensics team. Maybe my brother isn't a complete moron. Despite the relatively small mess made last night, the cleaner was in here for hours and was confident by the end of it that every trace of blood and brain matter was gone. At least now if the feds find a reason to search this place, they'll discover plenty of bodily fluid, but none of it criminal.

Still. The cocaine residue, the bevy of young female strangers who are probably in Vegas with fake IDs..., all we need is to get busted on a technicality, and Agent Lewis sounds like she'd be the type to play that game.

Caleb slaps the table in front of him. "What happened in Fulcort? You didn't call to update me."

It's going to be a long night. "Come get me when they've thoroughly swept for bugs and you've sobered up. We have shit to discuss." With that, I head for my room.

THE CITY below us bustles with life on this scorching August night, but up here on our terrace, the air is stagnant and mood somber.

"I've really gotta stop drinking." Caleb rubs his hands over his face. "For a second there, I thought you said *Dad* blew up our plane."

"That's because that's what I said."

Caleb stares at me in disbelief. "So, you're saying *our father tried* to *kill* us."

"No, he just wanted to teach us a lesson." I suck back a gulp of whatever Farley handed me in an attempt to cut some of the tension from my spine. An impossible task.

"A lesson. He wanted to teach us a lesson. He fucking *murdered* our best friends."

"And the crew," I remind him.

Caleb paces the length of the bar, his palm dragging along the smooth surface as he processes this news. But all I can think about is Mercy perched on that stool yesterday in her slinky electric-blue dress, its hem barely covering her thigh. I first laid eyes on her like that, right before I slipped her graduation gift on her finger—the diamond ring that's now sitting on the nightstand where she left it for the night, along with a silver bracelet and her phone.

The towel on the hook is bone-dry, but one of the robes is missing.

Bane was probably waiting for her when she stepped out of the bathroom. He didn't even let her get dressed.

"Exactly what lesson were we supposed to learn from this?" Caleb asks through gritted teeth. As I expected, he's seething.

"To watch our backs. We're too complacent."

He continues his route around the bar, whatever cocaine-induced high he was floating on earlier evaporated. "And Stanley told you this morning, but I'm only hearing about this now." His voice rises with irritation.

"We had *a lot* going on this morning," I remind him evenly. "What's the latest news on that, by the way?" The AM radio was buzzing the entire drive back. The reporters are speculating that the FBI presence at the murder scene suggests a connection to organized crime, but no names have been released yet. According to Stanley, the police have traced the SUV to Miles Perri and every faction of law enforcement presumes the charred, dismembered bodies are the infamous Perris in some sort of territorial war.

I turn to Merrick and Vince, lounging on the nearby couch. "No one's paid you a visit yet?" Considering these two are here playing "get the girls naked," I assume they have nowhere more important they need to be.

"They have. We told them we're not our brothers' keepers, we didn't travel here together, we're not in the same hotel, and we haven't seen or talked to them since yesterday afternoon." Merrick slides a pack of Marlboros from his jacket pocket and tucks a cigarette between his lips. "And we asked them to let us know when they've ID'd the bodies." He seems to have digested the fact that he shot his own father. I can't say I blame him for doing it. Camillo ordered Miles to murder the guy Merrick was in love with. I can relate. If any harm comes to Mercy while in Bane's care, I'll walk into Fulcort, aim the gun at Vlad's skull, and pull the trigger, audience or not.

"You should have told me," Caleb mutters, still focused on our father's betrayal. He snaps a finger at Merrick and then holds out a hand, wordlessly demanding a smoke. For once, Merrick doesn't have a sharp retort. He simply holds out the pack and the lighter for him.

Caleb lights a cigarette and takes a long drag. "If I'd known, I could have gone to Fulcort with you today and snapped his fucking neck—"

"And how would we ever get any answers out of a dead man? *That's* why I didn't tell you." The last thing I needed was Caleb there. They can't tolerate being in the same room on the best of days. My brother wouldn't have been able to control his temper. He would have killed our father with his bare hands, or at least tried. "You don't think he gave Bane explicit instructions about what to do with her if something were to happen to him? We need him alive if we have any hope of finding Mercy before Bane carves her up into pieces."

Caleb pinches his brow. He's finally seeing the bigger picture. "And let me guess, he's going to keep her tied up with Sergeant Psycho while we get his precious Harriet back on track, like he's wanted all along."

"That's the gist of it. And apparently, anyone who might challenge us taking over is no longer an issue." I give him a meaningful look.

His eyebrows arch in surprise with that bit of news. "That was fast."

But we knew it was only a matter of time before Bane caught up with our uncle and cousins.

"And what about this alliance with Camillo that he was pushing for? Has he heard about that yet?"

"Of course, he has. Says he expected as much from you."

Caleb rolls his eyes. "*And*? Is he pissed?"

My eyes dart to Vince and Merrick. It would be so easy to slide my gun out and sink a bullet in each of them, and concede to our father's demand. We'd have more bodies to clean up though. If we keep piling them up in here, eventually no cleaner will be able to erase what we've done.

But it would also mean I've become the very thing I don't want to be—like Vlad, a cold-blooded murderer.

Vince stiffens in his seat.

"He said the job was only half-done, didn't he?" Merrick says through an exhale.

They're smart, I'll give these two that much. I hesitate over how honest I should be. "Our father wants to take over your territory and he thinks eliminating you two will make it easier to do that. He's also waging a war against Navarro. He's got something planned. He wouldn't tell me what it is though." We could probably hunt down Ivan and JJ, another one of my father's dependable minions, and find out if we *really* wanted to. Whatever he's got cooking, those two will have their spoons in the pot.

"The old man has lost his marbles." Caleb chuckles bitterly. "And you told him to go suck Chops's dick because there's no way in hell we're on board for any of this, right?"

The more Caleb speaks, the happier I am I went to Fulcort alone. "No, I didn't say that. I played along to buy us time, and we'll keep playing along with big red bows around our necks until we can find Mercy. Do you understand?" My own anger and desperation bleeds through my tone. "I'll do *anything* to make sure Bane isn't given a reason to hurt her."

"Anything?" Vince's gaze flitters to my hand, and the proximity of it to my gun. The dangerous gleam in his eye and the way his fingers twitch tells me he's weighing his next move.

Merrick, though still lounging, looks like he could spring to action at any second too.

We're quickly sliding back onto thin ice with these two, as far as trust goes. The air is growing as tense as it was that first night they strolled into the office at Empire in Phoenix with their offer of this unorthodox alliance.

Caleb, sensing the volatility, edges in. "No. We're not

backstabbing shitbags like our uncle. Us taking over your territory is a stupid idea, made by a desperate old man who can't handle not being in control."

"As long as he has Mercy, he *is* in control," I counter. Does Caleb not see that?

My brother curses. "Listen to me, Gabe. Let's make one thing clear: we're not giving Vlad what he wants, no matter what. Because once we start that, it'll never end. Not until we're in Fulcort-grade jumpsuits or buried in the fucking ground!"

He's right. I know that in my head, but my heart is twisted into a thousand painful, anxiety-ridden knots. "But he can't know that."

"No, he can't," Caleb agrees, sucking on his cigarette. "We have to play along until we find out where Bane has stashed her."

"I've got Stanley working on it."

"That's good." He frowns in thought, then nods toward Merrick. "You, and all your intel…. Any idea where our father's favorite hitman holes up?"

"Never bothered to ask." Merrick shrugs. "But I can see what my sources can dig up."

"Yeah. Do that, would ya?"

Merrick opens his mouth—likely to launch a sharp retort—but then, as if thinking better of it, presses his lips shut. Still, his curious gaze lingers on Caleb as my brother paces in thought. I don't know what those two got up to earlier in the games room with all that cocaine and pussy, but if it's anything like last night's festivities by the pool, I'd say Caleb has somehow complicated this tepid alliance between our two families.

Vince is watching me carefully. He's still on edge. "Until you find her, how do you suggest we play along with the idea of you two *murdering* us? Because you know Vlad is waiting for a report on a fresh body count and my guess is he won't wait too long."

"No, he won't," Caleb agrees.

Our father isn't a patient man. Knowing him, he has Bane on standby with a backup plan.

But the look in Vince's gaze now is calculating. He's assumed as much.

"Don't do anything stupid," I warn. Like have Vlad executed in prison.

The bitter smirk that touches Vince's lips tells me I've hit the mark. He pulls himself out of his seat, standing tall. As if preparing. "Look, I get that this woman means something to you, but you're suggesting we sit around and wait for our personalized bullets to arrive and that's not a plan either of us are signing up for."

A fresh wave of anxiety slides down my spine. The remorse I was feeling earlier is quickly evaporating, my hand shifting closer to my weapon. "If *anything* happens to our father before I find Mercy—"

"Everyone, relax." Caleb's hands are in the air as he shifts into the space between Vince and me. "We're going to spin this in whatever way we can to keep Vlad thinking he's getting what he wants. We know how to deal with him. We've been doing it for decades."

Given the events of the last few days, I'd say anyone could argue that we have no fucking clue how to rein in

Vlad, but I keep my mouth shut. The last thing we need is bullets flying around again.

Vince's shoulders sag a touch, as if Caleb's assurances are welcomed. Maybe they are. Maybe he doesn't want to kill us either.

I allow myself the slightest sigh of relief. "It's probably best you two lay low for the next few days."

Merrick sighs. "You mean not sit around in a Vegas hotel with you two?"

"Something like that. We definitely need to put distance between each other."

"And act like you care that your father and two brothers are dead. Maybe head home, go be with your mother." Caleb tips his head back and lets a puff of smoke out. It sails up into the night, shaped in an O. "God knows that hateful fuck Miles was a guy only a mother could love, but I'm sure she'd like to see her youngest sons right about now."

Regretful looks pass over both Perris' faces.

Farley steps out onto the terrace then. "Sorry to interrupt but the feds are on their way up. They're in the elevator now."

Caleb curses.

My stomach churns as we all share a look.

"They already got a warrant?" Merrick's brow is furrowed with doubt.

Farley shakes his head. "A special agent Kennedy Lewis said she has a few questions."

"*Questions*? You let her up because she has questions? With Mercy missing? What the *hell* is wrong with you?" The last thing I'm in the mood for tonight is the feds crawling up my ass. That agent's been trying to flip Mercy and now she's suddenly gone. How will this look, besides that Caleb and I did away with her?

"Questions are *fine*. Questions, we know how to handle," Caleb tries to pacify me with a hand on my shoulder. "Just her?"

"And another one." Farley's wary eyes dart to me. "They said it was about the plane."

"Yeah, sure it is." Caleb sighs, his eyes flickering inside to where Michelle sits on the couch next to a bandaged and healing Moe. "That's just a cover. Lewis is coming to check on her little pet, make sure she's still breathing. She was messaging Michelle earlier to see what was going on with this FBI informant we got tipped off about, so I fed her some bullshit about Felix being the rat." The muscle in his jaw ticks, like just saying those words is painful. "Didn't want them busting our door down to 'rescue' the mouse they threw into the pit of snakes."

Merrick, ever the calm and collected one, stands and stretches. "I guess we better deal with them at the door and then send them on their way."

I trail the others, my pulse pounding in my ears.

Caleb lags, eying me warily. "Gotta say, Gabe, I'm not used to being the rational one here. We're gonna get out of this but you've gotta start using your head."

"If I was up here and not babysitting your ass downstairs to keep you from gambling our lives away, Bane wouldn't have gotten his hands on her."

"We both know that's not true." He scowls. "And stop acting cagey, like you got something to hide. Get your shit together before you give this agent a reason to haul us in."

The chill of the air conditioning engulfs my body as we step inside and head for the penthouse entrance.

"You." Caleb points to Michelle. "Sip your drink and keep your mouth shut. If you tip this agent off in any way, your friend's death is on your head, you got that?"

Michelle sucks back a gulp of her martini in answer.

The elevator dings and I brace myself for the performance of a lifetime.

A woman with tawny skin and black curls steps out of the elevator with her chin raised a notch too high. Her dark brown eyes flitter over the penthouse, doing a cursory search. They stall on Michelle, sitting on the couch next to a pale Moe, and her chest sinks with a barely noticeable sigh. Of relief, likely. Caleb was right. It's the only sign of vulnerability in that shield of confidence.

"Gabriel and Caleb Easton," she declares. "I've heard so many things. How nice to meet you both." At least she doesn't insult our intelligence by coupling that lie with a smile. She takes another step in.

"I'm a little rusty with protocol, but isn't this the part where you introduce yourself and hand us a warrant?" Caleb moves in to block her, his arms folded across his chest.

"Special Agent Kennedy Lewis. This is Special Agent Brock Williams." She waves her hand at the tall, lanky suit behind her. "And, yes, *if* we were here to search the premises. Is there a reason for us to search your rooms?" Her easy tone matches his.

"Nah. We're just a couple of guys enjoying what Vegas has to offer." His eyes rake over her body. She has the kind of curves that my brother tends to admire—ample. A full grip when he's driving in from behind.

Please don't hit on the FBI agent who wants to put us in jail, you neanderthal.

If she senses where his thoughts are going, she doesn't seem the least bit uncomfortable by it. "I'm no expert, but I believe Vegas has more to offer if you leave your room." She shifts her focus to the bar. Her perfectly drawn eyebrow arches. "Vince and Merrick Perri. Funny seeing you two here. I thought your families didn't get along."

She thought, my ass. She's read every file about the decades-long Perri and Easton feud backward, forward, and upside down. She knows exactly what happened—what Uncle Peter did to Nonna Perri, and the retaliatory hit that left our mother's body in a ditch. She and every other fed on the case knows it, but no one can prove it.

And I'm guessing she's wearing a wire, given she's making a point of naming all of us as her male partner stands by silently, taking visual inventory of all he can see.

Caleb folds his arms across his chest. "The older generation had some bones to pick, but we've made peace and here we are now, holding hands and singing kumbaya."

"You drove all the way to another state because you have information on who blew up our plane?" I'm unable to muster a leisurely tone. Besides, I'm tired of this act. It's a waste of valuable time that I could be using to search for Mercy. "Is that typical?"

"We do what we must to get to the truth." Her penetrating eyes graze over Michelle again—I'll give Mercy's friend credit, she's playing her part well, keeping her focus glued to the drink in her hand. "You're all in such fine spirits. Seems odd, given someone tried to kill you two nights ago, and *you two*—" Her eyes flip to Vince and Perri— "are waiting to hear if the bodies our forensic team is analyzing are those belonging to your father and brothers. Is *that typical*?"

"What can we say? We've learned to take these things in stride," Merrick retorts calmly.

"Maybe we're just in denial," Vince adds, stone-faced.

"*What do you want*, Special Agent Lewis?" Normally I'm a master at easy-go-lucky with the authorities but there's nothing easy about this inner turmoil swirling inside me. I feel Caleb's warning glare burning into the side of my face, but I ignore it. This agent tried to turn Mercy against me. She cornered her, terrified her, threatened her.

I know she's only doing her job, yet my fists curl at my thighs, my rage percolating with every second I focus on that.

She studies me a long moment.

Can she sense my hatred? My urge for retaliation? But she didn't win, I remind myself. Mercy didn't bend to her. She was ready to protect me.

"We have reason to believe Peter Easton was

involved in the incident at the Phoenix private airfield two nights ago."

"Uncle Peter? My godfather?" Caleb gasps. "*Never*! What makes you think that?"

"A source in our investigation." Her lips twitch as if she's struggling to stifle her smirk at my brother's theatrics.

Her source is Mercy. She mentioned it to the agent last night in the restroom, back when we believed him to be the culprit. Back when Mercy was desperately searching for any way to turn this agent's attention from me.

To help me.

"You'll have to ask Uncle Peter," I say coolly. "If what you say is true, he's not going to admit it to us."

"Well, you see, that's the problem. We haven't been able to find him. No one has seen him or his family in days. Seems odd that he would disappear at this time." She cocks her head. "Would you happen to know where he might be?"

"No idea. We left to come to Vegas hours after the 'incident'"—I use her word, which isn't much better than my father calling it a "lesson"—"and we've been here since." *As the tails on us could confirm.* I'm sure they noticed Farley and me slipping out of the hotel today and returning many hours later. It won't take them much to find my trail to Fulcort, if they look.

Agent Lewis's full red lips purse, as if she's considering her next words carefully. She pulls out her notepad. "There were four of you who escaped the explosion. You two, and a Miss Michelle Banks." She turns to Michelle. "Would that be you?"

Michelle swallows hard. "Yes, ma'am."

Lewis's gaze lingers on her another moment as if waiting for a cue before returning to her notepad. "And a… Mercy Wheeler." Her eyes flitter about. "Did she come with you on this trip as well?"

Lewis doesn't give a shit about the plane or Uncle Peter, who's probably in a deep, sandy hole by now, along with his sons. She's here because she was checking up on both her little mice.

"I don't remember you at the airfield the night of the explosion," Caleb says, and I appreciate the stall because I can't seem to conjure a lie fast enough.

"I'm sure you don't remember half the faces around you that night; you would have been in shock. But I was assigned to the case after. Is Mercy Wheeler here in Vegas with you?" She presses.

"She is. She hasn't been feeling well since we got here, so she's resting, and I'm not about to wake her so she can tell you that she has no clue where a man she's never met is. Now, if you don't mind, you've interrupted our evening and it sounds like you have some bad guys to hunt down."

Agent Lewis's lips purse as she glances at Michelle—perhaps to confirm the truth of that claim—but then she shifts her attention to her partner. "When do you plan on returning to Phoenix? In case we have more questions and need to contact you again."

"We check out tomorrow." Caleb grins. "Unless the roulette table's good to me and I decide to stay."

"Good luck with that, gentlemen." With another brief glance around, they leave.

Caleb waits until the elevator doors close before he announces, "She might need a bit more work before she falls for my insatiable charm."

"Don't worry, I'm sure you'll get another chance at her and soon." Because it won't be long before she comes sniffing around again.

Especially when we leave Vegas tomorrow, and Mercy isn't with us.

SIX
MERCY

My heart pounds as I watch Bane set a paper plate and fresh bottle of water on the floor. It's been hours since I last saw my captor. The blood-drenched apron is gone, and his cropped hair is damp from the shower I heard running on the other side of the wall earlier. He's changed into a fresh pair of blue jeans and an avocado-green T-shirt, and his leather boots are polished. All in all, he looks like any other man, save for the jagged scar that runs along the side of his face, as if someone dragged a knife down the length of it.

It's been hours and the woman hasn't screamed again.

"Hope you like peanut butter. It's all I got." His voice is grumbly, harsh. He seems annoyed.

I swallow but keep quiet. I haven't thought about food once since I woke up in the back of the van, and the white-bread sandwich he's left out like a dish for a dog doesn't stir any pangs of hunger now.

Bane's stony gaze rolls over the coral blouse and

white capris that I dug out of the suitcase. Whoever these clothes belonged to, she was a petite woman, older in years, based on the compression garments and modest style, who had a penchant for silk in bold shades of pink. The top stretches tight across my chest and the pants reach just below my knees, but it's a far better option than the heavy terry cloth robe. That, I've spread over the mattress so I have something relatively clean to sit on.

Much to my dismay, there was nothing else useful in the suitcase beyond clothes. No toiletry bag with nail scissors, no curling iron. Not even a belt. Nothing I could fashion into a weapon. I assume he made sure of that before he handed it to me. He doesn't seem like a fool.

Bane wanders over to the bucket and peers inside. "What are you, a camel?"

I bite back the lie that I don't have to go. The truth is I'm sitting on this mattress because after downing two bottles to keep hydrated, my bladder is ready to burst. Just the sight of another water bottle is causing me discomfort, but I can't bring myself to squat over the bucket yet.

"When will you call Gabriel again?" I need to hear his voice. I need to know he's coming to get me out of here.

"Who says I am?" Bane snorts. "Don't go gettin' your hopes up for some big rescue, doll. He won't find you out here. We're in the middle of nowhere and that ain't no exaggeration."

I take a calming breath, struggling to hide the fear

from showing on my face. "I think you're underestimating him. He's pretty resourceful."

"Oh yeah? And how long have you two been rollin' around in the sheets? A couple nights? A week, maybe?" He chortles.

"Longer than that." And in our time together, there's nothing Gabriel hasn't gotten that he wanted, including me.

"Sounds like he's been pouring all kinds of sweet lies into your little ears." Bane leans against the doorframe with a smarmy grin. "He's got you fooled *real* good. Don't you know what they are?"

"I know what his father is," I say coolly.

"Yeah. An Easton, just like Gabriel's an Easton, and that hotheaded brother of his is an Easton. Their kind don't give a damn about *anyone* but themselves and all their money. I know 'cause I've been doin' work for that family for way longer than you've been his little plaything, and you want to know how many problems I've solved for them in that time?" His eyebrows arch in question.

"You mean for his father?" This guy works for Vlad Easton, not Gabriel and Caleb. He said so himself when they were arguing on the phone.

"If that's what you wanna tell yourself." His lips twist in thought. "I should enlighten you to the things they've paid me to do to people—"

My head is shaking vigorously before he finishes his sentence. He's lying. Gabriel's never hired Bane to do anything that requires an apron and a shed in the desert.

He smirks. "Yeah, you ladies never want to hear

about that part of the business, do you? Takes the shine off all the diamonds, don't it?"

I instinctively reach for my finger. It's naked, the costly Paloma ring Gabriel gave me as a graduation gift left behind on the nightstand.

Bane's eyes drag around my room. "Yeah, I'd get used to this room if I were you. Vlad ain't in any rush to let you go, not as long as he can keep his boy in line by havin' you here."

"So, what, then? You're going to keep me locked in this room, bringing me peanut butter sandwiches every day?"

Bane shrugs. "Until enough time passes, and Gabe moves on. But you should know, I ain't good at keeping things alive. That's the opposite of what I'm good at doing."

I feel the color drain from my face.

His chuckle is dark as he shuts the door.

I barely notice the medley of locks clicking, my thoughts stuck on his words. Gabriel has been trying to get out from under his father's thumb for years and he's been making plenty of dangerous moves to ensure that happened lately. But now Bane has me, and I know why: Vlad is going to use me as leverage to force Gabriel into taking over the family drug business.

How long before Gabriel realizes that I'm not worth the power his father now holds over him?

"Who is H. G. Wells." A moment later, Bane hollers with glee. He's gotten yet another answer correct.

I toss the bland peanut butter sandwich back onto the paper plate. *Fantastic.* I'm being held against my will in the middle of nowhere and my captor is a wannabe Jeopardy champion. It must be late into the night by now, this is the fourth episode, and I've been sitting by the door, listening intently, hoping for some clue as to where he's holding me. So far, there has been no sign of other people, no visitors, no one has called, and Bane hasn't called anyone else.

"I'll take Stupid Answers for eight hundred, Alex!" Bane mimics the contestant.

Alex Trebek died of cancer last year. These episodes are definitely recorded.

After my little crying fit earlier, I got back to my feet with renewed vigor, reminding myself of what I went through with that lecherous prick, Fleet, and my father's ensuing murder conviction. Life felt hopeless for a time, until Gabriel came along and solved my problems.

He'll save me from this mess, too.

But if he doesn't, I have to be ready to save myself.

I dissect my tiny room in vain for the umpteenth time, strategizing escape routes. Even with a crowbar, I wouldn't have luck prying the plywood off the window. The door has too many locks and they're all on the outside. There's the light bulb, of course. When I flip the bucket upside down and stand on my tiptoes atop it, I can *just* reach the bottom of it. I'd have to shut the light for a bit, let it cool, and then unscrew it in the dark.

I could break it and arm myself with a piece of jagged glass.

My mind keeps veering back to that idea, but it's quickly followed by the worry: what if it doesn't break properly and I'm left with too small a piece to cause any real damage? I doubt Bane will replace the light and then I'll be left sitting here in darkness. As bad as being trapped in a room is, being in a dark room would be worse.

In any case, my bucket is full of urine now, stalling me from that desperate plan.

I could lie in wait by the door and swing the suitcase at Bane's head....

No, a flying suitcase won't take out a guy that got through Gabriel's security team with such ease.

The game show breaks for commercial and a loud creak sounds, followed by the shuffling of feet coming this way.

I scurry back to my spot on the mattress and listen to the locks open. Bane strolls in, dragging his boots as if tired from a long day. He heads straight for the pail.

My cheeks flush as he carries it out without a word, leaving my door wide open to disappear into the bathroom. Is this a test? Is he wanting to see if I'll make a run for it? My blood pounds in my ears as I listen to liquid splashing into the toilet. I clammer to my feet, the urge to try for an escape overwhelming. But how much of a head start could I really make before he caught up to me? What would he do to me?

It's dark out now, the glow from the sun around the

edge of the plywood gone. I have that going for me if I run. Probably the only thing going for me.

Before I can make a move, the toilet is flushing and Bane is strolling back in, dropping my bucket on the floor.

With a disinterested glance at my uneaten sandwich, he turns and leaves, locking the door behind him.

I WAKE WITH A START. It takes only seconds for my mind to register the mattress and the dull light bulb and the plywood over the window, and remember that this nightmare is real, not imagined.

An eeriness hangs in the stale air. There's no halo of light around the window to hint at daytime, so it must still be the night—

"No! Don't!" A man's shout echoes through the otherwise silent night.

I hold my breath and listen for more. Could it be Gabriel? Could he have found me and been caught by this psycho?

A scream sets the hairs on the back of my neck on end. There's no mistaking the sound for anything other than what it is—agony. That can't be Gabriel. Vlad wouldn't have his own son tortured, not when he's gone to the trouble of kidnapping me to force him into servitude.

"Stop! Please!" The man begs, followed a moment later by a panicked shriek. "We didn't talk! We didn't tell them anything! Tell Vlad we didn't talk!"

It's not Gabriel. It's a voice I don't recognize.

Didn't talk to who? Didn't tell them what?

Bane has clearly been paid to play judge, jury, and executioner, exacting whatever punishment his boss has ordered, with the assumption they've wronged him somehow.

Another pain-filled scream carries into the night.

And then another.

And another.

And another.

Nausea churns in my stomach, my hands reach for my mouth to stifle my own cry. I don't know who the man is or what he did to earn Vlad's wrath and Bane's attention, but no one deserves to suffer the way he's suffering.

The agonizing screams carry on into the night. I press my hands to my ears and hum to try to drown out the sound, until my throat is raw and the screams have shifted from blood curdling to sob laced to hollow, and then faded into silence.

But the memory of them lingers long after I hear the heavy footfalls trek down the hall, the running shower turn to a trickle, and the bedframe creak in the room next to mine—a murderer collecting his rest after a busy day.

He killed two people today, while I've sat in this room.

How long before I'm screaming like those people?

A SLIGHT GLOW of predawn light outlines the plywood, the only source of light in my room, as footsteps approach along the hall. Between the fingers of my right hand, I hold the shattered lightbulb. Several jagged corners jut out from the base. I grip my bucket between both fists.

Somewhere between Bane climbing into his bed and now, within the long, creeping silence, tangled in my horrified thoughts, I concocted this plan. It came easily, a domino of ideas. I walked through it a few times, practicing. A dress rehearsal of sorts.

But now, I fear I've gravely miscalculated a basic step thanks to my delirium. I have no idea if it'll work, and too many things could go wrong. Still, after listening to that man beg for his life, I have to try. Try, and pray I'm too valuable to Gabriel's father for Bane to harm me if I fail.

Blood pounds in my ear as I listen to the methodological click-click-click-clicks of the locks that secure my door. Four locks. Always fumbling. I recall seeing keys on padlocks the last time he came in.

My door swings open.

I hold my breath.

"Time to wake up." Bane grumbles, his own voice groggy. He reaches in to flick the light switch.

A bubble of terrified excitement bursts inside me. It's what I'd hoped for.

I fling the bucket, aiming the slosh of urine at his face before I drop it upside down on his head.

He yells in surprise but recovers in an instant, reaching for me, another move I'd anticipated—and hoped for. I slash at his hand with the shattered lightbulb. The angular glass slices across his palm, earning a hiss of pain.

I shove him from behind so he stumbles farther into my room, and then I pull the door shut and fasten the lock bolt at the top.

"You little bitch!!" He hurls himself against the door. "You think you're so clever, don't you!"

With trembling hands, I fumble with the three other locks—another bolt and two metal latches, the padlocks hanging open, keys inside—but the entire frame is shaking too much with each slam of his body against it.

"You just wait until I get out of here." His maniacal laugh skitters down my spine. "You're gonna be sorry."

A crack sounds, like wood splitting. He's going to break this door down any second. Abandoning the other locks. I turn and run down the narrow hall, and plow out the door.

The sun is just cresting over the horizon, blanketing the desert in an orange glow and dissolving the night's indigo sky. In any other situation, it would bring back fond memories of early mornings with Gabriel, on top of his mountain, lying on the loungers.

I quickly scan my surroundings. The security gate is closed and latched with chains. If I can get through that, I can follow the road as far as it will take me.

I run for the van, the sand refreshingly cool against my bare feet, and jump into the driver's side. And curse. The keys aren't sitting in the ignition, where I hoped they'd be.

A splintering crash sounds somewhere inside the

trailer and my stomach drops. Bane must have broken through the door.

I slam my hand down on the van locks to buy myself time and then fumble in the console, in the cup holders, anywhere someone might leave a set of keys.

I find them in under the sun visor.

From the corner of my eye, I see a form charging my way. I force myself to ignore him and focus. I'm *so close* to being free. But my hands are shaking so bad when I try to slip the key in the ignition that I drop them on the van floor. "Shit!" I scramble to collect them.

That's when the driver's side window shatters.

I scream as a bloodied hand reaches through to hit the lock switch. In seconds the door has flung open, a fist is roped around my bicep, and I'm yanked out of the driver's seat. I struggle to stay on my feet as Bane drags me back toward the trailer.

"I've been nice, haven't I? I've brought you water and food. Haven't laid a finger on you," he mutters more to himself. I fight against his grip, but he's strong, shockingly so for a wiry man. "And what do I get in return? Covered in piss and sliced up!" His rage echoes through the quiet desert. "Apparently I've been *too* nice. It's time we rectify that."

He's not taking me back to the trailer, I realize. We're heading toward the garage.

To the place where I'm almost certain he's killed two people since he brought me here. God only knows how many before that.

A fresh wave of panic seizes me. I can't let him take me in there.

I twist and turn, kicking at his shins as hard as I can, first with my bare toes, then with my heels, trying to break free.

"Settle down!" He punctuates the warning with a backhanded slap across my face that sends my head snapping to the side.

Pain explodes across my cheek where his knuckles make contact. I take a moment to breathe through it as he hauls me closer to his torture room, a limp in his step now. "No problem, my ass. Fucking Eastons. Told Vlad I don't wanna deal with this kind of shit. He said you'd be no problem. Bullshit."

The metallic taste of blood touches my tongue. I ignore it as I scramble for desperate words. "You *can't* kill me. Vlad needs me alive if Gabriel's going to do what he wants."

"Good thing there's a long way to go between alive and dead. You're about to find that out."

I struggle against his grip again. It earns me another hard slap.

While I'm recovering from the blow, Bane jams a key into the door's deadbolt.

Inside the garage is pitch-black and reeks of chemicals. Bleach and I'm not sure what else. Within the path of the early morning light that streams through the doorway, I see nothing but a big, open space and a chain that dangles from the ceiling.

And a small table with various tools laid out in a tidy row.

Almost surgical.

Bane drags me forward, toward them, his fingertips digging into my flesh and muscle.

My heels scrape across the dirt floor as I resist. "I'm sorry! I won't try anything like this again, I swear! It was a mistake!"

"Yeah, I've heard that before, once or twice." Bane snorts, clasping a handcuff that was on the table over my wrist. "I promise, you won't be trying that again after this."

I let my legs buckle, hoping my deadweight will make things more difficult. But, despite my best efforts to resist, he has my wrists bound above my head in seconds, and attached to the overhead chain.

I tug against the bindings, only to confirm that it's secure. "What are you going to do to me?" I can't hide the fear in my voice as I eye the various blades, pliers, and other tools. How many people has he used those on?

"Seeing as I've gotta go fix your door, I thought I'd leave you in here for a while." He yanks on the chain, pulling me up onto the balls of my feet. "Let you learn firsthand what a bad idea it is to get mixed up with an Easton." Strolling toward the door, he flips a switch near the door. A light flickers on, casting a dim glow over the vacuous space. "See you in a few hours." He slams the door shut behind him, leaving me dangling.

I allow myself a sigh of relief. As uncomfortable as I'm going to be soon, at least he's not using those tools on me.

Yet.

Hidden beneath that strong chemical smell, I note

something else. A mixture of scents—sickly sweet and pungent and foul. And yet there's nothing much in here from what I can see.

Plenty of yellow fly tapes dangle throughout, speckled with black dots—the corpses of winged creatures. Otherwise, the garage is empty, save for a few oil drums and a tidy row of shovels and saws. I count six of each. How many shovels does one man living alone in the desert *really* need?

I guess it depends on how many bodies he buries out here.

I shudder at that thought.

"What'd you do to end up here?" A voice calls out, startling me.

I ease myself around on the balls of my feet in search of its owner, somewhere behind me.

When I see what occupies the back corner of the shed, my mouth drops open, but the scream is silent.

SEVEN
GABRIEL

We left Phoenix only forty-eight hours ago, and yet as we stroll into the palatial foyer, the marble floor gleaming from a fresh mop, the house feels hollow, abandoned.

And the comfort I was feeling being within these walls lately—the ease of coming home to my bed and its occupant—no longer exists. I won't ever feel it again, not until Mercy is with me.

"Meet your new sidekick." Caleb makes a dramatic bow and gesture, as if introducing Moe to Michelle for the first time. "You eat, you sleep, you tinkle in the toilet…, he'll be there. You need soap rubbed on your back while you shower, he's your guy. Understood?"

Michelle, who stared out the passenger window the entire drive home without saying a word, nods furtively.

"You try to leave, signal for help, or try *anything at all*, Moe will tell us, and trust me, you don't want us finding out that you've tried to fuck us. *Again*." He punctuates that warning with a savage glare that doesn't take too much effort on his part. He's in a pissy mood after leaving Vegas without controlling ownership of the Mage—our whole reason for the trip in the first place. My father's list of unsavory demands is just extra sauce on top of a shit sundae.

Michelle swallows, her eyes darting to the mute, stone-faced bodyguard who carries two bags despite the bullet wound he earned twenty-four hours ago. "I'm not going to try anything. I want to help find Mercy. Anything I can do. *Anything* at all."

"That's the spirit!" Caleb claps his hands together dramatically. "For now, make yourself scarce in my wing, where you'll be sleeping. Pick a room. Any room but mine. Gabe and I have things to discuss." He flutters his fingers in a farewell gesture and then heads for the bar, dismissing her. Farley and the rest of our security team fan out over the property.

I check my phone for the hundredth time, for news from Stanley that he's located them, for a missed call from an unknown number that could only be Bane, allowing me a chance to hear Mercy's voice again. Still nothing. Not that I would have missed either.

I feel this overwhelming urge to scream, and keep screaming until I know she's okay and this deep ache inside me finds a moment of respite.

"Alright Gabe. I've followed you along for the ride up until now. Tell me you've got ideas for how we're going to win against dear old Dad."

"I've got ideas." It's *all* I've been thinking about since I left Fulcort yesterday, when I'm not thinking about Mercy. How do we kill Merrick and Vince, and scare

Puff into compliance without *actually* doing *any* of it? And how do we manage all this with that FBI agent in our shadow?

Our first hurdle—hiding from Agent Lewis the fact that Mercy didn't leave Vegas with us—was solved care of Becky, one of Caleb's showgirl friends who has the same body type and long dark hair as Mercy. She arrived last night with a gaggle of women and stayed over, agreeing to dress the part—in one of Mercy's outfits, wide glasses, and a low-brimmed hat. With my arm around her and her face nuzzled in my neck, the short walk from the elevator to the SUV was easy enough.

But I know Lewis's type. She's a lot like the agent who took down our father, a total dog on a bone. She'll eventually figure out that Mercy isn't in Phoenix with me and, when she does, she's going to assume the worst happened—and that I'm behind it.

We'll deal with that when we get to it.

Caleb sets his Glock on the counter and pours two glasses of vodka. "So, let's hear 'em. How exactly are we going to convince that snake in an orange jumpsuit that we're committed without getting ourselves or Mercy killed in the process?" He downs his in one smooth gulp and nudges the other one toward me. "Both of which are highly likely, by the way."

"By getting on board with what he wants." It's the only way. I leave my glass where it is, untouched. I need all my wits about me if we're going to pull this off.

My phone chirps with a text. It's like a fire drill in my pocket. I rush to grab it.

Stanley: I think I figured out what Vlad had planned for Navarro.

His message is followed by a link to a Mexican news source, written in Spanish, with pictures of a charred building.

I thrust the phone into Caleb's face. "What does this say?" My Spanish is mostly nonexistent, save for a few phrases I use with our housekeeper, Rosita. It's certainly not good enough to decipher this.

He squints as he reads the screen. "A lab outside Hermosillo was hit last night. Looks like they were slicing and dicing cocaine, and someone lit it up bigtime." He lets out a low whistle. "Seven dead so far, the warehouse torched. Go big or go home, I guess."

I sigh heavily. Hermosillo is in Sonora. "That's Navarro's territory." Our father must have been working that angle for a while now, long before Navarro's guys hit Puff's crew. Finding out one of those locations is no easy feat. I'll bet he pulled it out of one of Navarro's guys on the inside in Fulcort.

"So he has Ivan or JJ torch the guy's operation and now he wants us to go on like everything's copacetic? The guy's going to cut us down the second we step out of our house." Caleb laugh-snorts, as if the idea is preposterous.

But nothing about this is funny. The reality is, Navarro will retaliate and soon. "We've got to keep up appearances until Stanley tracks down Mercy."

He sighs heavily. "How far *on board* are we talking here? Are we Rose or Jack in this situation? Are you

Rose and I'm Jack? Cuz I don't wanna be Jack. Things didn't work out too well for him."

Leave it to my brother to make a stupid joke during a serious conversation. Except maybe he's not too far off this time. "We both fight like Rose and hold on like Jack, until this whole fucking dirty empire goes down, once and for all." And if Mercy isn't in my arms when it's all said and done, I'll sink to the bottom of the ocean along with it.

EIGHT
MERCY

I SWALLOW against the taste of bile that lingers at the base of my throat. The two bites of peanut butter sandwich I dared ingest earlier sit in slimy clumps on the dirt in front of me, heaved from the depths of my digestive system. A few chunks landed on my silk blouse, splashed onto my toes. If I vomit again, it'll be on an empty stomach, and there's nothing worse than retching on an empty stomach.

Except doing it while you're chained up by your wrists, hanging in a torture room, awaiting your turn.

"You're wearing my mother's clothes," the man says, drawing my attention to him despite my desire to look away.

And he's wearing none. He's been stripped and shackled to a chair, his ankles tied to each other, allowing for no modesty, not that he seems particularly embarrassed given his situation. His wrists are bound and pinned against his chest by a chain, sitting just below a barbed metal collar. I can only assume the series of chains binding him are set for tension. His unnaturally stiff posture and the countless streaks of dried blood that stain his skin say he moved at some point and learned a painful lesson.

"He gave them to me." I clear the rough patch from my throat. The growing ache in my arms is quickly taking over the pain in my cheek. "He didn't tell me whose they were."

The man's brawny chest rises with a deep breath. He must be in his mid-thirties. Short, based on how he fills the chair. And muscular, though strength didn't keep him out of his predicament, and it won't help him now. "That's okay. She doesn't need them anymore."

So, Bane did kill that woman. I thought as much.

"I'm sorry." I hesitate. "Was that her I heard yesterday?"

"Yeah." A grim look passes across his face. "He killed her yesterday. Killed my father the day before. And my brother, Alexei, was late last night. Or maybe it was this morning. The psycho took an extra long time with him, so I can't be sure. He did it all right where you're standing. I'm all that's left now, and he's going to kill me, too." There's no fear in his voice, just matter-of-fact words. He doesn't look like the kind of guy to not put up a fight, but the fight's certainly all gone now. Maybe that's what happens when you watch your entire family tortured and murdered.

I resist the urge to search the dark corner for the heap of carved flesh, for fear of heaving again. I couldn't see all the ways Bane tortured this man's brother, but stumps where fingers and toes used to be is enough to know our captor is far viler than I ever imagined.

He enjoys inflicting pain.

"Why is he doing this to you?" I ask.

"Because of my fucking cousins. They're the ones who set this in motion. They wanted us gone." The muscle in his jaw ticks, the first sign that he's anything but listless. "And there they were, pretending they didn't care about the family business, but I guess it was all an act to get us out of the way, so they could take over everything. They knew what would happen if Vlad found out who really put him in jail."

Familiarity burns in my memory. I've heard this story before, but a different version of it. "You're Gabriel's cousin." And his father was Gabriel's uncle. "Your father blew up our plane." They have to be one and the same.

"We had nothing to do with that!" The guy erupts, then grits his teeth. Crimson drops bloom where the barbs are digging into his flesh. "That was Bane. That was *Vlad*."

"But…." I frown. *Gabriel's father tried to kill us*? Why try to kill his sons if he needs them to run the business?

"Doesn't make sense, does it? Except it does to Vlad. Guy's a heartless bastard. A lesson for his sons, because he's tired of Caleb and Gabriel dicking around."

"So, he blew up their plane? With their *friends* in it?"

"Welcome to the Easton family, where everyone is expendable. Vlad ordered it and his psycho dog set the bomb." The guy pauses to take a few breaths, as if breathing through the pain. "He admitted to it all before he executed my father."

I knew Vlad Easton was a terrible man but to do something like this? Does Gabriel know his father is behind all of this yet? Or does he still think his uncle is the one who set the bomb?

I'm reminded of something else Gabriel told me. "Didn't your father work with the FBI to put Vlad away?" That would explain why Vlad had Bane kill him. Or is that a lie, too?

The guy's lips twist as if considering his answer. "Vlad was growing too arrogant, making too many risky mistakes with the business. Creating enemies. Personally, I would have solved that problem with a bullet, but my dad couldn't bring himself to kill his own brother. Betrayal and jail, he was fine with. What can I say? My old man's logic might have been skewed as much as Vlad's. They were cut from the same cloth, after all. Anyway, I'll bet he was regretting that choice in his last moments, 'cause Vlad certainly didn't feel the same." He pauses. "Which one of my degenerate cousins has been talking about private family affairs with you? I thought they knew better than that."

A twinge of paranoia stirs inside me. There is a lot that Gabriel has yet to divulge. He's always guarded his tongue when it comes to how his family has made their fortune, but our "don't ask, don't tell" rule is dissolving as we grow closer. He did say that telling me anything about his family's criminal enterprise would put me in danger.

What would his father do if he found out Gabriel's been revealing things to me?

Would he consider me a threat?

"Let me guess…, Caleb's incapable of human connection beyond where he sticks his dick, so you *must* be Gabriel's."

I remain silent.

"I never expected to see Gabe hooked by a woman." He pauses. "But now you're here, which means Vlad ordered it. What's that about? I doubt he disapproves. Vlad's a family man, after all. He'd want to see his bloodline continue, especially given he's killing us off." His eyes drag over my body. "So, what's his beef with you?"

Despite this man's unfortunate predicament, I'm having a hard time feeling sympathy for him. He certainly isn't showing me any.

He smirks at my continued silence. "What are you worried about? Who am I gonna tell? You're the last person I'll ever speak to. I'm the last person *you'll* ever talk to, besides that lunatic out there."

"No, Bane can't hurt me," I blurt out. "He's not allowed."

The corner of his mouth twitches in amusement as if he's in on a secret I'm not privy to. "And why not?"

I hesitate. "Because Vlad's using me to force Gabriel to do what he wants. If he hurts me, he'll lose the control he has over Gabe."

The man's tired eyes drift over the length of my body again, from my bound wrists all the way to my bare feet and everywhere in between, stalling on the popped button in my shirt. "I don't think Bane got that memo."

My cheek is swelling from the backhanded slaps, but I'm guessing that discomfort will soon be nothing in comparison to the burning in my arms and calves. How long will Bane keep me like this? A few hours? I can't imagine that. "It could be worse," I say instead, my eyes flickering to the mutilated body in the corner.

"It *will* be worse, trust me. Bane kills; that's what he does. That's all he knows how to do. As soon as Vlad decides you're a threat, he calls Bane. He decided my family was a threat." A haunting look passes through his eyes.

"Were you?"

"We were gonna cut them out of the business," he confesses after a moment. "Vlad's in jail and my cousins are too busy playing party boys in their club to do what needs to be done. Why the hell should they keep getting an equal split of the profit without taking any of the risk? So, we were gonna take it all. I warned my father that leaving any of them alive was a bad idea, but he was too stubborn to listen to me. Says he knew his brother better than I did." He shifts, and winces from the barbs. "And now Vlad's eliminating us. His own blood. And once Vlad gets what he wants from Gabe, he'll get rid of you, too. But knowing Gabe, he'll decide you're not worth all this trouble and he'll tell his dad to fuck off. That could happen any day. Then there'll be no point in keeping you alive, and he'll give you to his dog as a play toy."

An unsettling feeling blisters inside me. Bane said

something similar. They're both wrong. I *do* know Gabriel and he would never leave me here like this, even if this guy is right and Gabriel trades his freedom from his father for me. The man I used to believe to be a lecher does have morals and decency. He won't let me die like this. "No, Gabriel will find me before that happens."

"Look, I'm sure you're a nice girl. Stupid, for falling for my cousin, but nice. So let me fill you in on a little secret, because I've known my cousin for a lot longer than you have. He discards women like used tissues during flu season. He's probably sitting in his mountaintop house right now, checking his speed dial to see who's available, seeing as you're… hung up at the moment." He snorts at his own joke but then winces.

You deserved that one. "I've spoken to him and he's looking for me." I struggle to keep the indignation from my voice.

"Gabriel Easton doesn't give a damn about anyone but Gabriel Easton. He looks out for number one. That's why I'm here."

My anger flares. "No, you're here because your father ratted out Vlad and put him in jail. He betrayed his brother." And apparently Vlad's vengeance is vicious and far-reaching.

"And do you think Gabriel and Caleb care that Vlad's behind bars? They're happy he's locked up. They fucking *hate* their father. Anyone with two eyes can see that. My father did them a favor by putting Vlad away. They *should* have been kissing his ass when they found out how Vlad ended up in there. But no, for whatever reason, they decided they wanted their entire family slaughtered. Who knows why? Maybe they've been playing us all this entire time, waiting for their chance to swoop in and take it all. They knew what Vlad would do if he found out. They knew he wouldn't stop at his brother. That psycho killed my mother, and brother, too." His voice catches, the first real sign of emotion. "But this way, they get to keep their hands clean. Then all they need is for Vlad to die. Who knows, maybe they've already got a plan to kill him, too. They're conniving bastards."

Gabriel admitted as much to me—that he knew his father wouldn't let this betrayal go unpunished. But is it true that he and Caleb knew the ramifications to his entire family? To his aunt and cousins?

The guy studies me. "Then again, maybe I'm wrong. Maybe Gabe *is* head-over-heels in love with you and going out of his mind, suffering right now, knowing you're in Bane's hands, and not knowing where you are. Thinking about the kinds of things he's going to do to that body. Actually, I think I'll die happier with that scenario running through my head."

I'm seeing why Gabriel has no love for his family. "He'll find me." I say that as much for myself as for this asshole.

"Women tied to this family don't fare well. Don't believe me? Look at the track record. My aunt Virginia, my mother…, both dead, and brutally."

"Both because of something *your* father did," I throw back.

The muscle in his jaw ticks. "You're right, my father

is to blame for all this. And he was a fool for thinking he could reason with Vlad. I didn't make that same mistake though."

Dread courses through me. "What do you mean?"

He bares his teeth in a thin, pained smile. "Let's just say that when the sun sets on this family, *no one*'s getting what he wants."

NINE
GABRIEL

"SHE JUST CAME BACK from taking the child for a walk," Farley confirms.

"And security detail?" Puff must have someone watching over his baby mama now that he's reneged on the arrangement with our family. He's not stupid. He knows Vlad isn't happy with him and he knows the kinds of things that happen when Vlad isn't happy.

"One skinny kid on the steps, his head in his phone. He won't notice us until it's too late."

One kid who's gonna regret not taking his job seriously. "And neighbors? Witnesses?" We're doing this in broad daylight.

"We won't give them anything tangible to go on." Farley's confidence in his men is unwavering. I wish mine was as steadfast, but after they fucked up and let Bane take Mercy, they're all amateurs in my eyes. There's a pause. "Are we a go?"

The nausea in my stomach over what we're about to

do churns. This is Vlad's arena. "Do it. And send me confirmation as soon as you have it." I end the call.

We don't have a choice. We have to play his game. That's the only way I'll ever see Mercy again. I remind myself of this for the tenth time as I climb out of my car. "We're rolling."

"So are our friends in Cali." Caleb grinds a cigarette butt into the pavement with his shoe. "They're not thrilled about it, but they said they'll do it."

"They're not thrilled with *staying alive*?" Caleb and I agreed that the best way to deal with Dad's request to eliminate the two remaining Perris is if they go underground until we tell them it's safe to pop their heads back up. I'll bet Vince is the one complaining about playing dead so he doesn't end up actually dead. He seems like he'd be the type to complain about something as stupid as that.

Caleb answers with an eyeroll before shifting his focus to the looming gates of Fulcort. "Sooner this is done, the better. I really hate this fucking place."

Three minutes later, my phone chirps with a text from Farley. My stomach twists as I hold it up for Caleb to see.

"They say a picture says a thousand words." He turns away, revulsion curling his lips. He doesn't like this any more than I do.

"Yeah, well, this one says it's showtime." Let's just hope this production goes off without a hitch.

Every guard in this room has a cozy spot in Vlad Easton's pocket.

Not the Easton family pocket.

Not *my* pocket, like Donny.

They're all Vlad's minions, paid to keep him as safe and secure as any inmate can be in this fucking hellhole. But to have them all in here now? He's pulling a lot of levers. He must be worried about retaliation—from Puff's gang, from the remaining Perris, from Navarro. Who knows? It's coming from all angles. He's been making too many enemies as of late.

Frankly, the only reason his own sons haven't killed him is because he has something—or someone—we want.

The guards were the first thing I noticed when I sat down at our usual corner table.

The second thing was that it was dead in here today. The waiting room is full as per usual, but it's just us and Caleb in here now.

It's probably for the best, given what's about to go down.

Dad drums his fingertips on the table in a steady rhythm, his steely gaze wandering across the room to the table where Caleb sits, waiting. There's no way Caleb doesn't feel the eyes boring into the back of his head, but he doesn't acknowledge him in any way.

Also for the best, given how they parted ways the last time—fists cracking bones—and that was *before* we knew the truth about the plane explosion.

"Saw the news from Sonora. I take it that was you?" I ask, keeping my tone bored.

Dad smiles. "I think our friend might hesitate before striking back this time, now that they've received our message."

Not our message. Your message. And they're going to strike back twice as hard.

"Eduardo has agreed to doubling the shipments going forward."

My eyebrows arch. "*Doubling*?"

"How else are we going to accommodate our new territory?" He asks, as if I'm an idiot. "I've given Eduardo your number. He will contact you directly about future shipments."

"Fucking great." Because that's what I want to be getting: texts from a cartel drug lord.

This is all happening too fast. I feel like I'm getting sucked into a black hole. And Dad? He's in his glory, grinning like a madman as he dictates.

"When Eduardo does call, you will answer. If he asks you to meet with him, you will go wherever he expects you to attend, promptly, otherwise he will consider it a personal insult. I don't think I have to explain to you what will happen if Eduardo feels personally insulted."

Probably the same thing that would happen if Vlad felt insulted. It begins with a phone call and ends with a sharp blade and a shovel. "I hope he gives me enough time to get there, now that some asshole blew up our plane."

"Watch your mouth," Dad snaps. "Who do you think you're talking to?"

I smirk. The audacity. After all this, he *still* demands my respect.

"You need to make sure our new territory is *fully* secured before the next shipment arrives."

I have until then to kill Merrick and Vince, he means. "It's in the works, but I don't know if it can happen that fast. People are more cautious, given events of late. Plus, we're having some *legal* issues after your lesson. You know, on account of the four people who died in that explosion? And those legal issues are crawling up our asses now, asking all kinds of questions."

"So, you tell them your uncle Peter is behind it." He chuckles, as if he just made a joke.

"That's the going story." I choose my next words carefully. "But they have a witness list from that night and they're looking for Mercy. They want to question her, and they think it's odd that they can't find her." If my father knew the feds were trying to turn Mercy, she'd be dead inside the hour.

Dad shrugs. "So, tell them she was nothing but a piece of ass that got spooked. Not your problem."

"That's what I've told them."

"Then there's no problem."

Wrong. There's a huge fucking problem. "I want to hear from her."

"You did."

"That was yesterday." I keep my tone calm but razor-sharp. A lifetime ago, it feels like. And today, I have so much I have to say to her. "I need to know he hasn't harmed her in any way."

"And what if he has?"

"You better hope he hasn't."

My father studies me through calculating eyes for a long moment. "I can see that you truly care about her. Maybe as much as I cared about your mother."

"Oh yeah?" *Isn't that why you had her kidnapped, you fucking prick?* I ball my fists tight to keep from reaching across the table and choking him. "And what would you have done to the guy who kidnapped my mother, if you'd had the balls?"

Before he has a chance to erupt, the door opens and Puff strolls through with his typical swagger as if he doesn't have a care in the world. Meanwhile, his head's practically on a swivel, doing a cursory glance around the room. All these guys do. *I* do it, too. We're criminals; it's in our nature.

When he sees who occupies the room and the situation he's just landed in, he visibly stiffens.

"Buddy! It's been too long!" Caleb exclaims as if greeting an old friend. "Come on over and take a seat." He gestures across from him.

Puff is a scary-looking motherfucker on a good day, the scaly dragon tattoo that occupies the entire left side of his face the stuff of nightmares. Now, as he eases over, his steps measured, his hands flexed for a fight, he reminds me of a cornered animal ready to fight for his life.

"That pompous ass. *You* should be having this conversation with Puff," my father murmurs. "You'd be far more effective."

"Caleb will be plenty effective."

He offers no more complaints, settling in with his arms folded on his belly to watch as Puff slides into his seat and Caleb leans in for their little tête-à-tête. This is how Vlad likes to operate—with a smarmy "I warned you, didn't I?" look on his swollen face as he watches his underlings dole out his punishment.

I steel my expression as Caleb pulls his phone from his pocket and brings up the pictures Farley sent us earlier—of his baby-mama and child, tied up and blindfolded in the back of the van, terrified. With a thumb swipe, he shows him the next picture, from Farley's West Coast guys, confirming how they strolled into Mama Puff's sunny little San Bernardino home and likewise escorted the elderly woman out.

Every muscle in Puff's neck tenses a second before he lunges for Caleb with a roar.

Caleb, expecting the reaction, is quick on his feet, moving just out of reach. Likewise, the guards expected something was about to go down because three of them dive in, grabbing Puff by his arms and slamming his face onto the table.

"You're all dead!" He screams through bared teeth, his cheek against the metal surface. He struggles against his restrainers, but they have a solid grip of him. "Every single one of you is dead!"

I know exactly how you feel, Puff.

"Did you just threaten us, inmate?" One of the guards—a steroid-filled beefy dumbass named Mills—glances at the security camera aimed in their direction. The tiny red light cuts out abruptly. He takes that moment to pin Puff's right hand on the table and then he pulls out a hidden baton and smashes it against Puff's knuckles.

I grimace at the sound of bones cracking.

Caleb waits until Puff's grunts of pain to quiet before he leans forward, closer to Puff's ear. "Do we have an understanding?"

After a moment, Puff spits out a contorted "yes."

"I'm glad you see it our way. Pleasure doing business with you. Gabe'll be in touch very soon." Caleb pauses to give our father an "are you satisfied?" stare but doesn't wait for a response, sauntering out of the visitor's room.

He plays the part well; I'll give him that much. Wouldn't guess he didn't enjoy that power. But I know he's as nauseous as I am about this whole deal.

"That hand's not looking good, inmate. You sure you don't know how it happened?" Mills exclaims with mock-concern, his weapon out of sight. Two guards haul a seething, hunched Puff out the door. They'll dump him in his cell and wait until tomorrow before they suggest visiting the infirmary, so they can mark it down as a prisoner dispute in the paperwork. Throw a bunch of inmates together and they break bones all the time. And they don't talk.

Moments later, visitors begin trickling into the room and the guards shift back to their watchful posts.

Dad nods toward where Puff and Caleb were sitting. "Let's hope that's the last time we have to have a conversation with him about his obligations to our family."

If all goes well, that'll be the last time there is any

talk of obligations to the Eastons. "On that note." I rise. "Call Bane. I want to know she's okay."

"Sit down," he barks. "We're not done with our conversation yet."

As much as I want to tell him to go fuck himself, cooperating will get me farther. Still, I wait a few beats before I settle back into my seat, my ass perched on the edge, primed for liftoff.

"The new fish has made a lot of *very* protective friends." Dad's smile doesn't reach his eyes. It never does. "Did you think I wouldn't notice you trying to flex in here?"

He's talking about Mercy's father and the ring of influential prisoners I've thrown bills at. Between them and the few guards I trust, the man is never without a shield. Not in the chow hall, not in the courtyard, not even in the showers.

"I don't give a shit whether you notice," I lie. If he's been paying attention to that "nobody," as he once called him, it's not for any good reason. He's strategizing, and Mercy's father is a sitting duck.

Dad opens his mouth to retort, probably to call me on my lie, but decides against it. "Expect a phone call from Eduardo. Maybe tomorrow. Maybe next week. But whenever it rings, you answer it."

"I guess that depends on whether my phone rings today, doesn't it? And it better be damn well ringing by the time I get back to my car."

He grits his teeth. "Bane is loyal but difficult, you know that."

"But you're so good at making people do what you

want them to do." I lean forward, meeting his gaze. "Twenty minutes or maybe I'll be too busy to answer the phone when Eduardo calls, and he can be personally offended."

I leave Vlad seething at the table, but my mind is spinning. If I somehow find Mercy—no, *when* I find Mercy—my dad will just shift his focus to her father, and if something happens to him....

Donny meets me in the hallway near the waiting room. He jerks his head and leads me into one of the small private rooms. It's the room I carried Mercy into, the day she passed out at the security desk after finding out her father had been beaten to an inch of his life. Back when she was merely a conquest for me. "You still want me to toss his cell for that phone?"

"No. Wait for my text on that." Something tells me Dad has more shit up his sleeve, and it involves tightening this noose around my neck by targeting Mercy's father. "I want Chops moved into Duncan Wheeler's cell, immediately."

"Oh man." Donny curses under his breath. "I don't know how to make that happen, Gabe—"

"Figure it out!"

"Do you know what it took to get Chops his own cell?" He hisses, glancing around. "And now you want me to snap my fingers and undo that?"

"I don't care. Wheeler doesn't sleep, eat, or shit without Chops standing over him and one of *you*"—I jab him in the chest with my finger—"*s*omeone loyal to *me*, within three feet at all times. And if a single hair gets plucked from that guy's head, so help you God…, your mother, your sister, your sweet little nephew, Blake…."

Donny swallows. I don't need to finish that threat. He knows I'm good for it. "It'll take a few days."

"Get it done." With that, I storm out, second-guessing everything we've planned so far.

TEN
MERCY

EVERY MUSCLE in my body burns like I've been pricked with a thousand scalding needles. My skin is raw where the handcuffs have dug into my wrists against my sagging weight.

"Ooh-wee!" Bane exclaims in his gruff voice, strolling in. "It's sure gettin' ripe in here."

It's been hours since Bane left me with Vic, Gabriel's cousin. The overwhelming smell of bleach from this morning has given way to the putrid stench of rotting flesh and bodily fluids. I've taken to breathing through my mouth to keep from gagging.

"How're you doin'? Hangin' in there?" He tips his head to peer at my face. "I'll bet you're regretting that little stunt you pulled earlier, huh? You got somethin' to say?"

He wants me to apologize, to beg him to cut me down. A guy like him would. I already apologized for running, but I won't beg. I set my jaw and fight the tears that threaten.

"Hmm. So that's how it's gonna be." His lips purse in thought as he regards Vic. "Okay, then. Let's give you a little taste of what might happen if you ever throw a bucket of piss at me again." Bane collects a long metal rod from the table.

Panic seizes me. I don't know what it is, but it can't be good.

He passes me and continues toward Vic.

Apparently, Vic knows what it is. He tenses, the reaction causing the collar around his neck to dig into his flesh. He grits his teeth from the pain as he watches Bane flip a switch.

"My daddy used one of these cattle prods on us when we didn't listen to him. Hurt like hell." He yanks on a chain and Vic's arms fly up over his head. He screams as the barbs dig tight against his flesh, and then again when Bane presses one end of the prod against his armpit.

"He only ever had to do it once to me. I learned my lesson. Now, my brother, he was not the sharpest tool in the box." Bane's tone is easy, conversational. "He was an arrogant and stubborn son of a bitch. He kept getting into trouble, and our daddy kept giving him lessons. You remind me a lot of my brother, Vic. That's why I saved you for last. It's gonna be fun breaking you." Bane shifts the prod down and slides it between Vic's legs.

Vic buckles, trying to shift away from the weapon. Blood pours freely from his neck wounds where the barbs keep digging with every twitch.

"Stop it!" I cry out. I don't like Gabriel's cousin, but no one deserves this.

"Aww, how cute. Did you two bond while I was away? You think this guy would beg me to stop if it were you in his place?" Bane snorts. "He wouldn't say a damn word. Hell, he'd probably make me strip you down, and he'd get a little chubby from watching. Wouldn't ya." He sends another electric current through Vic's scrotum.

Vic's face turns red as he grunts, trying his best to stifle his screams. But the tears that slip down his cheeks betray him.

"Stop it! You sick fuck!" I shriek, the agony in my muscles forgotten.

"What? You don't believe me, do you? How 'bout we find out then." Bane pulls away from Vic and moves toward me, the end of the prod aimed at the patch of exposed skin on my stomach.

I use whatever strength I have left to brace against the impending pain.

In the quiet lull, a phone rings.

"Oh, what the hell does he want now?" Bane tosses the cattle prod to the dirt floor, and slides a phone from his jeans pocket.

I allow myself a shaky sigh of relief.

"What," he barks by way of greeting. "Yeah… yeah…." Bane's sharp gaze flips to me and he scowls. "Yeah, she's a real fucking peach, just like you promised. Already tried to escape once."

That must be Vlad.

"No… no… I told ya, I ain't a fucking concierge—"

Vlad yells into the phone, his words unintelligible but severe.

Bane's lips purse. "Yeah, fine." He ends the call, all

his bluster gone. To Vic, he mutters, "Guess we'll get back to you once you've had a minute to recharge. Wouldn't want you expiring too soon." He releases the chain holding Vic up, allowing enough slack that the wounded man slumps in his seat, the spiked collar loosening.

"Time for you to go back to your room. For now, at least." Strolling over to me, he unfastens the chain from a hook.

I drop to the floor in a heap, unable to keep myself up.

Bane leaves me to lie there a moment, reveling in the feel of cool dirt against my cheek, before he nudges me with his boot. "Come on. Get up."

"I can't." There's no strength left in my body.

"For fuck's sakes." He hauls me up and over his shoulder with surprising ease. I don't even consider attempting to struggle as he carries me back to the trailer, to my room, where he tosses me onto the mattress.

The light bulb has been replaced, this one duller than the last, and he's nailed a sheet of plywood to the door, to cover the hole he put through it to get out.

"If you want to talk to your darlin' *boyfriend*, sit your ass up," he grumbles, disappearing for a moment only to return with a phone and a scrap of paper. He reads off the number and starts hitting keys.

He's calling Gabriel. I'll bet that's what Vlad was demanding. I struggle to drag my limp body into a sitting position, leaning against the wall for support, as Bane dials.

"You get a minute, and no funny business or I promise ya, it'll be the last time you ever talk to her," he says by way of greeting and then he's thrusting the phone into my face.

I swallow. "Gabriel?"

His deep, raspy sigh fills my ear and it's like a balm to my aching muscles. I close my eyes a moment and try to block out my current situation, try to pretend we're tangled within his silky sheets next to each other. "I'm going out of my mind here, Mercy. You have no idea. God, please tell me you're okay? Tell me he hasn't hurt you?"

It's basically the same questions he asked last time, in that same desperate angry tone. He's afraid for me. Probably because he knows what Bane is capable of. Maybe because he's hired him to hurt people like this before, too.

No, I can't think like that. I can't let Bane and Vic get into my head. If I do, I won't survive this.

What would Gabriel do if he knew Bane strung me up like a side of beef and left me hanging for hours? That I was seconds from being electrocuted with a cattle prod when his father called? "I'm okay." I'm not dead, I remind myself.

"Is he standing right there?"

I peel my lids open to find the wiry psychopath hovering over me, checking his watch. I don't know what he's so worried about. I can't tell Gabriel a single thing that will help locate us. "Yes."

"Can he hear me through the phone?"

"I don't think so." I hesitate. "I met your cousin. Vic."

"Yeah, I knew Bane had them. What about my uncle?"

I steal another wary glance at Bane. He doesn't seem concerned that I'm divulging that bit of info. "Dead. So is your other cousin. And your aunt."

A few beats of silence answer me and then, "Don't worry, my dad wants you alive. You're no good to him dead."

"Bane said there's a long way to go between alive and dead." I look up and the asshole winks at me.

Gabriel curses. "I'm not going to let anything happen to you. I swear, I'm doing *everything* I can to keep my father happy while I look for you."

What does that even mean? What kinds of crimes does Vlad have him committing? "Don't do something you can't undo on my account, Gabriel."

"I'll do *whatever* I have to. Anything and everything, do you hear me? No one else matters to me but you." Sincerity bleeds through his voice.

But will he ever find me, is the question. According to his cousin, it won't be in time, whatever that means. With Bane looming, I can't say much. "My father—"

"He's safe. I won't let my father get to him."

I was going to say that my father will be expecting to see me today. "What do you mean? Why would Vlad go after *him*? He's got me." My father has nothing to do with Gabriel. A fresh wave of dread rolls through my body. After all that I've done to keep him safe from Fleet in Fulcort, now he might have a bigger target on his back and again, it's because of me. "Gabriel, if something happens to him—"

"We don't have time to get into it, but he's protected. At least, he will be soon. I've made sure of it. But I need you to tell me what Bane was driving. Yes or no answers, got it?"

I falter, but force myself to focus on a spot on the floor, rather than check Bane's face. "Yeah."

"Was it a van?"

"Yes."

"Dark colored?"

"No."

"So it was light. Was it white?"

"Time's up." Bane barks, holding out his hand.

"Yes. I miss you, too," I tack on at the end. There's an ache in my chest, an overwhelming feeling that I may never hear from Gabriel—or anyone—ever again. I know I'm testing my captor's patience but I rush to add, "He's keeping me in a single-wide trailer and there's a big garage with a green tin roof—" My words cut off with a howl of pain as Bane slaps the phone out of my hand, catching my injured lip in the process. It goes flying across the room, hitting the wall.

"Mercy!" Gabriel shouts through the speaker.

Bane picks up the phone and ends the call without another word. "You think you're so clever, don't you? You think you can help him find you?" he snorts. "Well, I've been doin' this a long time, sweetheart, and I can promise you, he don't have a hope in hell of finding you. And even if he gets that PI of his to track this place down?" Bane leans in close to me. "I'll make sure he sees me slitting your throat before he ever gets through the gate. And then I'll string him up and gut him like a fish."

"You can't." Tears trickle down my aching jaw. "If you hurt him, Vlad will kill you."

"And how's Vlad gonna do that? He's behind bars, and I'm the guy he hires to kill guys like me! You think his merry band of goons can do it? There's a reason he uses me for the big jobs. Those fools wouldn't last a day trying to hunt me down." He sneers. "But I warned you no funny business. Just for that, you're gonna get some more time in the shed. Tomorrow. Tonight, I've got work to do an' I don't need to hear your whinin' in the background. Takes the fun out of it." He turns on his heels and marches out of the room, but pauses at the door. "And that's the last light bulb you're gettin'. You mess with that and you'll spend the rest of your days in the damn dark." With that, he slams the door shut and latches it.

I rest my aching body on the mattress and focus on the single water bottle that sits next to yesterday's peanut butter sandwich, less the two bites I vomited in the shed when I saw the mutilated body in the corner.

Is Bane right? Is the only way I'm leaving this place going to be to end up in a hole in the desert?

And if he tortures Gabriel....

No, that won't happen. I'm going to get out of here.

I tell myself that repeatedly, and push aside thoughts of what horrors await me tomorrow.

Exhaustion finally pulls me into sleep.

ELEVEN
GABRIEL

"Bane won't kill her. He can't," Caleb reassures me as we stroll past three of Farley's men and toward the front door. Our place is crawling with security—a necessity given all the flaming balls we're juggling. We're Enemy Number One now, as far as Puff is concerned, not that he'll do anything while his mother, girlfriend, and child are being held hostage in an undisclosed location. And then there's Navarro. For all we know, his men are on their way here to exact revenge for what my father pulled.

"*He hit her.*" My jaw clenches at the memory of that cry she let out just before the phone went dead.

"She'll heal. And she'll say it was worth her getting a few licks if it helps us find her."

"Since when are you the pragmatic one," I mutter. The little bit that she gave us *was* helpful. Stan identified a white van with Nevada plates—registered to a woman who died ten years ago, no obvious connection to Bane—and was able to use recorded security feeds to follow it onto the interstate, heading northwest. It's a start, but we're a long way from zeroing in on a location with a green metal roof.

And I can hear Mercy saying just that.

But I can just as easily hear her telling me to fuck off and die, and never come near her again after this ordeal. She'd have every right to.

Caleb reaches for the doorhandle, and frowns. "What is that sound? Is that *barking*?" He opens the door and steps in cautiously.

Inside, a scraggly long-haired chihuahua scuttles across the cool tile floor of the foyer.

"Why is there a *dog* in our house?" Caleb hollers.

"It's hers." Farley nods toward the terrace where Sasha Rosado and her two-year-old son, Puff Junior, sit at the edge of the pool. She has a protective arm around his body and seems to be doing her best to ignore the security guards that hover around them.

I sigh with relief. That's a better look than gagged and teary in the back of a van for Puff's benefit. His reaction had to be genuine in order for our father to buy it.

When I told Caleb that we were going to bring our hostages here, he burst out laughing. Until he realized I was serious.

"We said woman plus child, not woman plus child plus this… this… rat." Caleb grimaces as the dog runs up to his shoe and starts sniffing. It has more bald spots than actual fur.

"There'd be no one there to feed it. What if it starved to death?"

"*And*?"

Farley's brow furrows as his gaze shifts between Caleb and the five-pound ankle biter, trying to figure out if Caleb is serious. Obviously, Farley has a soft spot for four-legged creatures. Amusing, given I've seen him break the legs of plenty of two-legged creatures over the years.

I roll my eyes. My brother's issues with dogs go all the way back to age six, when one similar in size sank its teeth into his thigh. The scars are faint but still there. "It's fine."

"Jesus. As if this day hasn't been bad enough." Caleb heads toward the bar. The dog trots behind him.

"How are they?" I nod toward our guests.

"Scared."

To be expected. Five big guys busting down your door and dragging you out of your house tends to do that.

"And the others? How far away are they?" San Bernardino, where Puff's mother lives, is at least a five-hour drive from here.

"An hour out, tops."

I sigh with reluctance. "Okay, I need to call Puff then, and fill him in on the plan."

"I guess that leaves me to welcome our guests." Caleb sizes up the stunning brunette from above the rim of his glass for the first time, a familiar glint of interest in his eyes. "Damn. She's a hundred levels out of his league. What's her name again?"

"Her name is 'mother of Puff's child and a supremely fucking bad idea,'" I warn. "We have a ton of smoothing over to do with him and *that* won't help. Stick your dick elsewhere."

Michelle strolls past us then, offering a tepid smile, heading toward the back terrace, her dutiful babysitter Moe trailing closely behind her. A red bathing suit dangles from her fingers. I assume it's for Sasha to borrow while she's here.

"My options are severely limited, thanks to you," he mutters, following her out.

I sigh. "Keep an eye on him, would you? I don't need him making this problem worse." It's bad enough already. I need to call Puff before he sets things in motion that can't be undone. He has plenty of allies in Fulcort and he won't take this lying down.

Farley's deep chuckles vibrates in my chest. "You have more to worry about for your brother than her. She's a feisty one. Got nails on her."

Shit. "Well, make sure he doesn't lose an eye, otherwise I'll have to listen to his whiny ass for the rest of my life." With that, I head for the privacy of my wing to make this call, hoping Puff has his burner on him and he's in a place where he can answer. I don't know what to say to ease his rage. I know what he's feeling right now and there's no forgiving the people behind it. I can only plead empathy. Trouble is, I don't know if a guy like Puff can spell the word, let alone show it.

Puff answers on the eighth ring.

"How's the hand?"

"Shattered," he grumbles, his voice laced with agony.

"Donny will get you patched up. You won't have to

wait until tomorrow. And he'll get you some good painkillers."

"Gee, *thanks*." Hatred spews from each syllable. "What the *fuck* do you want, Gabe?"

This is the part where Vlad Easton would demand respect.

"I want you to shut your mouth and listen very carefully to what I'm about to tell you, and maybe we'll all get out of this alive."

TWELVE
MERCY

I CLENCH my teeth and throw myself against the door for the tenth time. I don't know if I had any chance of breaking it down before, but with the plywood Bane nailed over the hole, it's hopeless now.

I sink to the floor, exhausted and afraid.

Vic is dead; I'm sure of it.

If he's not, he's wishing he was. I listened to him scream for hours, until the screams waned and then they stopped. Then the van engine came to life and took off. I assume Bane's gone to bury the evidence of his crimes in the desert using one of his many shovels.

Four people in three days. Soon, he'll have no one left to torture but me.

He's all but promised to drag me out there again tomorrow.

Good thing there's a long way to go between alive and dead.

I pull myself to my feet and slam my body against the door again, harder this time.

A ceiling tile shifts, revealing a space above.

My heart thrums with adrenaline. There's an attic of sorts, a space I might be able to fit through, if I can get up there.

I *have* to get up there.

I dump the contents of my piss bucket into the corner of the room and flip it over, then climb on top. It's not nearly high enough and even if I jumped and grabbed onto the edge of the wall, I wouldn't have the strength to pull myself up after what I went through today.

My mattress.

It takes all my effort to drag it over to the opposite corner and prop it against the wall. I climb slowly. But the mattress wobbles and sinks, and slides down to hit the floor, taking me with it. I land hard on my backside.

My frustration swells. If Bane comes back and sees that loose tile, he'll know I figured out a way out of here and he'll take it away from me.

This is my only chance.

I get back to my feet and shove the mattress in place, using the edge of the plywood against the window to keep it from sliding and the bucket and suitcase underneath to keep it from sinking.

It's on my fourth wobbly attempt that I manage to grab hold of the wall's frame. Every muscle in my body screams in protest as I haul myself up into the crammed space. It's a thousand degrees in here, pitch-black and musty from age. I'm not entirely sure I'll even fit. Still, I can taste triumph. I hold my breath and slither along the hallway, past the insulation and dust, trying not to consider what else might be living in here.

Suddenly the ceiling gives way under my weight. I tumble through and land on my back. Something heavy comes crashing down nearby, followed by a noisy clatter, like a bag of marbles scattering. I struggle to catch my breath, the wind knocked out of me for three beats.

All around me, the last dribs of sunlight shine a light on the dust floating in the air.

I'm in the hallway.

I'm free from my cell.

Exhilaration propels me forward. I drag myself to my knees, surveying my surroundings.

There's a gun. It must have been stashed in the ceiling.

I pick it up without thinking, trying to remember the meager lessons I've received from my father and from Gabriel. It's loaded, that much I can tell. The safety isn't on. I'm lucky it didn't go off.

I set the gun down and pick up a wad of twenty-dollar bills. There must be a hundred of them here. There are plenty of other bundles too, of twenties but also fifties and hundreds. I guess it's not surprising that a guy like Bane doesn't keep his blood money in a bank.

I take in all the bits of insulation strewn over the floor with renewed focus.

And frown. That's not insulation.

Those are bones. Small human bones. Fingers, knuckles, teeth. Some I can't identify.

There must be hundreds of them.

Horror clutches me as I take them all in. I'll bet these are all from his victims. Trophies he's collected over the years, of all his kills.

How many people has Bane murdered for the Easton family?

"What the hell?" Bane's voice startles me.

I let out a yelp as I look up to find him standing in the doorway, his jeans covered in dust from the desert. I didn't hear the boots on the steps or the door creak.

His lips split in a wicked snarl, the scar across his face pulling at his cheek and distorting his face. "What did I tell you would happen if you tried this shit again?" He charges for me.

The gun.

It's a fleeting thought, and then suddenly the cool metal is against my palm. I don't hesitate. I point the gun and squeeze the trigger.

A blast cuts through the night.

THIRTEEN
GABRIEL

"He and I have more in common than I first guessed," Caleb muses, his arms folded as he watches the toddler tear past the wall of glass windows. The boy shrieks with excitement as he checks behind his shoulder to see Sasha running behind, a fresh diaper in hand. We sent Moe out with Michelle to stock up on a few essentials, given Farley's guys didn't give them time to pack.

"Why? Because you've both run around the pool buck-naked with a woman chasing after you?"

He shrugs. "Basically. Except I've never shat myself."

"Yet."

His gaze wanders to the set of couches where Puff's mother is perched, calling her grandson to her with a broad smile and open arms, pajamas dangling from her fingers. It's all an act for his benefit. She's a sweet, tender woman in her seventies, five foot one and a hundred pounds. She's about as far away from what I pictured Puff's mother to look like as possible, and when Farley helped her out of the van and into our garage, and I saw the terror in her eyes and the way she clutched the cross around her neck, I wanted to vomit for my part in this.

"You know, she hasn't seen her grandson in eighteen months?"

"Puff isn't exactly a traditional family man." He's got three or four kids with different women back in California, and he's been incarcerated since before this one was born. But Sasha is the only one to visit him, and rumor has it she's "the one" for him.

"Neither are we. We've never had kids around here before." Caleb pauses, taking in the spread of food on the table that Michelle also took care of, enough to feed everyone. "It's nice though, you know?"

"Nice?" I can't help the bark of laughter that escapes. "They're *hostages* and they're surrounded by a small army of security."

"Still."

I'll admit, this *is* a nice change from the usual gatherings we host here, where there's still nudity but far less innocent. The little boy has been in and out of the pool all day, having somehow shed the terror from earlier, his laughter grabbing my attention each time it sounds.

And I've found myself watching them and daydreaming that it's not Sasha but Mercy, laughing as she chases a small child—our child—around this very same pool. They're ideas that have never crossed my mind before, and now I'm afraid they're ideas that will never transpire to the real thing.

"We're taking good care of them," Caleb cuts into my thoughts.

"Yeah, let's hope Puff sees it that way when this is all said and done." He didn't seem to relax when I explained what was happening and he sure as hell didn't seem to sympathize.

"Gabe," Farley hollers, the security phone pressed to his ear. "They just let Special Agent Lewis through."

Caleb groans. "She's like a tick that won't stop feeding on my ass!"

I knew this was coming, but I didn't expect it for another day or two. "With a warrant?"

Farley shakes his head.

"So, more questions." This agent is really getting on my nerves.

"I guess we're doing this outside then? Since we can't have her coming in *here*." Caleb gives a wide-eyed look at our "guests" before leading the way out.

"TWICE IN TWENTY-FOUR HOURS. WHAT A PLEASURE!" Caleb leans against the hood of his Porsche.

I match his stance, using my Lambo as a prop. Inside the garage, the two vans used in the abductions are tucked away.

"Short trip to Vegas for big gamblers such as yourselves." Agent Lewis's heels click against the pavement as she strolls toward us. The same silent blockhead agent that came with her to our penthouse trails her now, surveying his surroundings.

"Just a quickie this time. In and out. Then again,

two nights is about all I can handle of the place," Caleb lies.

"Still…. Vacation together, work together, live together." Her gaze rolls over my car, and I can't help but notice the appreciative flash in her eyes. She may be a pain in my ass, but Lewis knows a nice car when she sees one. "Can't say I've ever met brothers who are so close."

"We share women, too. Thought you should know that since you seem so interested in both of us," Caleb says with a sly grin, being… well, Caleb.

"I'll keep that in mind." Her responding tight smile doesn't reach her eyes.

"Awfully late to be paying a visit. How can we help you *again*, Agent Lewis?" I force a nonchalant expression. Inside though, I'm panicking. We're juggling too many balls as it is, and having this woman as an attentive audience while those balls are flying through the air makes things a million times more precarious.

"I thought you'd be more anxious to find out who blew up your plane, but you don't seem to care." Her sharp gaze drifts over the front of our house, taking in the security cameras. "Why is that?"

"Wouldn't want to steal your thunder. Solving crimes is your job, isn't it?" Caleb folds his arms over his chest. It's his signature relaxed pose. He's far better at this game than I am. Then again, ever since Mercy was taken, I've been dangling on a frayed rope. "I thought you said the going assumption was our uncle Peter."

"Yes, and yet we can't seem to find him or his sons,

your cousins Vic and Alexei. Or even Rita Easton. They've disappeared, and no one's seen them for days."

"They do that sometimes."

"And you haven't heard from them at all?"

"No. Like we told you just last night."

"A lot can change in a day." She reaches out to test a leaf on our acacia tree. It was one of our mother's favorites. "In our search for them, we discovered that you two were looking for your cousin, Vic, the night of the explosion. What did you want him for?"

A muscle in my jaw tenses. I hope they don't notice, but I think Lewis notices far more than most. I can see where this is going, though. The girls at Vic's seedy strip club must have talked, and now Lewis is attempting to weave a story that pins their murders on us. Wouldn't that be ironic.

"Wanted to invite him to dinner. It's been too long," Caleb answers without missing a beat.

"Someone bungles an attempt to kill you two and you're paying late-night visits to strip clubs to make dinner plans? Come on guys. Do you really expect me to buy that?" Her tone is patronizing.

Lewis is here in our driveway and not in an interrogation room, which means she has nothing on us, not even enough circumstantial evidence to haul us in. She's fishing, hoping we'll trip up.

"Obviously we didn't suspect our own family of trying to kill us," I add, tempering Caleb's flippant response. "But we're happy to see you so focused on our safety. Please let us know what you find out during your investigation, and if we have anything to worry about from them." It's a good thing Bane is an expert at what he does. Those bodies will never be found.

"You know what else I'm working through? Why you and your crew"—she glances at Farley—"ended up in Vegas at the very same time Camillo Perri and his four sons were there."

"Vegas is a popular destination. And, like you said, we're big gamblers. I've heard they like to dabble at the poker table."

"And it just so happens to be the same trip that someone murders three of them."

Caleb gasps. "Oh shit, is that *for sure* for sure?"

I ball my fists. I'm used to my brother's glib attitude, but I'm ready to strangle him.

"Not *for sure* for sure yet. It'll take time to identify the pieces. But all the preliminary evidence points toward it." She pauses, as if deciding what more to say. "Security footage shows Camillo, Miles, and Leo leaving their hotel on Thursday night, and based on various street surveillance footage, arriving at the Mage around ten p.m., pulling into the underground parking. It's interesting though, that the Mage's camera system malfunctioned around that time and remained down until the next day. Specifically the cameras in the garage and the service area elevators."

"Yeah, that place isn't run very well. We weren't impressed," I hear myself say. We knew if the feds dug, they'd find that oddity soon enough.

Caleb drops his voice to a mock-whisper. "Between you and me, the owner is going to run that place into the ground."

She smirks. "When did you two last see Camillo, Miles, and Leo?"

"Gosh. Years, I'd say. Years, right, Gabe?"

Before that night, yeah. "Probably since Camillo was on trial for murdering our mother. You remember that one? You guys fucked up the investigation and he got off on a technicality."

"You're right, he should have been put away for that, but it was the state police who botched that. It sounds like you still hold a grudge though." She watches me closely.

"Nah. Bygones. But they clearly pissed off someone. Good luck though. Sounds like you're up to your eyeballs in missing people and unsolved crimes."

"There *have* been a string of gang-related murders as of late. We assume they're tied to Luiz Navarro."

"Who?"

She snorts at my feigned innocence. "The leader of a drug cartel who our intel suggests has been working his way deeper onto US soil." She begins slowly pacing back and forth in front of us—three steps to the left, three to the right. "I imagine business has been challenging for all of you lately, what with Navarro picking off your distribution channels, one by one."

Caleb frowns. "I don't know what you've heard but our night club has been rockin' lately. We're up, what, 30 percent versus year ago, Gabe?"

"Thirty-two percent." My voice sounds wooden. They may suspect a lot, but they can't prove any of it and we all know it.

"Thirty-two percent! See? Business is good. We can't

speak for the Perris' wineries though. You'd have to talk to Camillo about that. Or, I guess Merrick and Vince now."

"Well, that's the thing. We've *also* lost track of Vince and Merrick Perri after we saw them in *your* penthouse. You wouldn't happen to know where they are, would you?"

In hiding, waiting to see if they have to stage their own deaths to keep this charade with Vlad going. "Probably home with their mother. That's where I'd be."

"That's what I thought but we've spoken to Gina Perri and she hasn't seen or heard from them. They never made it back from Vegas. She was worried that something might have happened to them, especially given what we suspect of the others."

We know for a fact that's not true. They were at Camillo's Napa Valley house when Caleb phoned Merrick and told them the plan. They've coached their mother well. I wonder, if our mother was alive, if she'd conspire with us like that. "What exactly are you insinuating here, agent? That we had something to do with them going missing *too*?" It's best if the rumor that Merrick and Vince have gone missing is floating around. It's likely to reach my father's ears.

"If you did, I promise you, I'll find out." She considers her next words. "There seem to be a lot of people going missing lately. Some, ending up dead. And they *all* have ties to you two."

"Coincidental."

"I don't believe in coincidence when it comes to criminals. There's always a link."

"Good thing then, last I checked, we've never been convicted of any crimes." My patience is thin tonight. I want her gone.

"I don't know about you, Gabe, but this is feeling an awful lot like an interrogation and given we're the ones who nearly died, I find that shocking. Are you accusing us of something, Agent Lewis? Should we call our lawyer? He can be here within ten minutes." Caleb's voice has taken on a hard quality. He's had enough of playtime, too.

Her throat bobs with a swallow. She knows she's pushed us as far as she can. "I'm looking for Michelle Banks and Mercy Wheeler. I know they both accompanied you to Las Vegas. I have some follow-up questions for them about the night of the explosion."

"We were all there together. What could they tell you that we couldn't?" Caleb counters.

"That's what I'm wondering. We've checked their residences and they're not there. Their neighbors haven't seen them. They both came home from Vegas with you, didn't they?" Her eyebrow arches in question, as if she is not 100 percent convinced of that.

I knew this was coming. My stomach clenches. "Mercy left when we got home. I have no idea where she went."

Lewis's gaze narrows a touch before she can smooth over her expression. "And Michelle Banks?"

"She's inside. I'll go and get her for you." Caleb casts a warning glance my way—reminding me to keep my cool—before disappearing inside.

Lewis and I are left alone outside, her mute partner lingering out of earshot.

Her lips twist as she studies me. "I heard you left the hotel yesterday morning and didn't return until last night. Where did you go?"

She's not even trying to hide the fact that they have surveillance on us. "Out for a drive."

"In Nevada?"

"Am I not allowed?"

"Of course you are, but you can understand why that would seem odd, right? Come to Vegas with your girlfriend and leave her at the hotel to go for a *long* drive. You did leave her in the hotel, right?"

"I told you already, she wasn't feeling well."

"Or maybe she was occupied by your brother. Seeing as you two share everything—"

"Not her," I snap before I can stop myself.

She crooks her head, watching me steadily. "So, she is yours."

"Yes." Mercy is mine. She has been since the moment I laid eyes on her. And I'll do anything to get her back.

"Then where is she? Because I wouldn't take you for the kind of man who didn't know where your woman was at *all* times. Especially so soon after someone tried to kill you."

"You obviously don't know me then." My phone vibrates in my pocket. As much as I'm itching to answer it, I stay my hand. It's not the phone I use for legitimate business, which means it's either Stanley, or Donny, or my father.

Or it could be Bane.

Lewis can't overhear any of those conversations.

"Maybe not, but I know your type and you're not at all unique. I know that Ms. Wheeler is scheduled to work on Monday, and she *never* misses a day. You know, her boss said she's only ever taken one sick day in all the years she's worked at that drug rehab center?"

Great. An FBI agent has been talking to Mercy's boss. It's not bad enough she's been abducted, but my shit is bleeding into all aspects of her life. "You seem to be very focused on my girlfriend. Why is that?"

We spend a few long moments in a staring match that tells me everything I need to know. Lewis thinks I found out she was trying to flip Mercy and killed her for it.

"Let's cut the shit. I expect to see Mercy at work on Monday and if I don't, I'll consider her to be a missing witness to a multiple homicide by a crime family. And the people in this house were the last to see her alive. You just confirmed that."

Monday morning. That's thirty-six hours from now. Will Stanley have found Bane's hideout by then?

The front door swings open. Michelle and Caleb stroll out, arm in arm.

"Caleb says you want to speak to me about the plane explosion?" Michelle asks, tucked into Caleb's side. It's all an act, but Michelle is playing along, her hand landing on Caleb's stomach affectionately. Behind them, Moe lingers, taking this babysitting duty far too seriously.

Lewis's dissecting eyes sit on her. "Actually, I think I

got the answers I needed. Have a good night, gentlemen." To me, she adds, "I *will* be back here, and it'll be with a warrant next time." She strolls toward the black sedan, her hips swinging with her steps, more swagger than even Caleb can muster on a good day.

We watch in silence as the car pulls away.

"She thinks I killed Mercy."

Caleb waves my words away. "She's got nothing. All guesses, no smoking gun."

"Doesn't mean she can't make our lives hell." My phone rings in my pocket again. A second call in as many minutes; it's important. I dig it out of my pocket. "Yeah?" I bark.

"Gabriel?" A woman's tentative voice fills my ear. "Is that you?"

My heart pounds in my ears. "*Mercy*?"

She sighs heavily. "Yeah."

I share a bewildered glance with Caleb. "*Where are you*?" The deep rumble of transport engines shifting gears can be heard in the background.

"At a small truck stop. In Nevada, I think? Or maybe California. I don't know. I see license plates for both. The diner's called…" Her voice drifts as if she's looking around for a sign. "Bobby Joe's."

It takes me a moment to process this. Is this *really* Mercy? Her tone is oddly flat. "Where's Bane?"

"He's dead. I killed him."

My jaw hangs open. The ex-military ghost who has been called unstoppable… got stopped.

By Mercy.

"I don't know how to get home. I just *really* want to get home. Please help me."

Her plea snaps me into action. "Shit, of course." I rush for the front door, for the keys to the Lincoln. "Are you safe where you are?"

"I think so."

"Okay. Stay there. I'm on my way to you."

"But you don't know where I am."

"Don't worry. Just stay there, and I'll find you."

And I'll never let you go again.

FOURTEEN
MERCY

"HOTEL CALIFORNIA" by the Eagles plays over the crackling speakers as I watch the familiar black SUV race toward the diner, a dust cloud trailing it. It's been hours since I made that phone call. The sky in the far east hints at predawn light. Morning can't be too far off.

I allow myself the first deep breath of relief in days, even as my hands tremble around my coffee mug. Gabriel found me, like he promised he would.

I'm safe.

When Bane discovered me sprawled out in the hallway and charged at me, I didn't think, I unloaded the gun on him—five rounds into his torso. I just kept squeezing the trigger and the weapon kept firing, until it clicked empty. Even then, I kept squeezing.

He fell hard, crashing into his television, taking the entire stand and its contents down before toppling over his recliner.

I remained frozen—sitting on the floor, spent gun in hand, surrounded by the tokens of countless victims—

for I can't say how long. It was probably only seconds and yet it felt like hours, staring at his slack face and the pool of blood soaking into the cheap vinyl floor. I didn't need to check for a pulse. His eyes told me he wouldn't be able to hurt me anymore.

And then, like a spark ignited in me, I couldn't get out of there fast enough. Without any thought I grabbed a wad of money from the floor and bolted toward the van. Only, the keys weren't anywhere in it this time. Back to the trailer I went, nausea churning inside my gut. I gingerly fished through Bane's pockets as if he were merely sleeping and not to be disturbed. I found the keys along with a phone.

To my dismay, the phone was dead. The last thing I wanted to do was drive out into the desert at night with no line to civilization, and yet there was no way I was staying in that compound with my dead captor and countless ghosts for a second longer. I found a charging cord on the kitchen counter, next to a scrap of paper with a scrawled phone number. I remembered Bane dialing the number on that paper to call Gabriel. So, I snatched the paper and the cord, and I ran out to the van again.

The drive out of Bane's secret hideaway was long and dark and bumpy, my knuckles white around the steering wheel. Half the time I wasn't sure whether I was on a path, or driving aimlessly through the desert, heading straight for a cliff. But eventually I came to a proper road. I followed that until I saw lights in the distance, which brought me to this remote roadside stop, where travelers come for a hot meal and to fill up the tank. By that point I had enough juice in the phone's battery and a signal to make a phone call.

There was only one I wanted to make.

Since then, I've sat in this booth for hours, ordering food I can't stomach and coffee I can't drink, listening to Gabriel tell me everything's going to be fine over and over again, our conversation interrupted frequently by signal issues and dropped calls.

The Lincoln comes to a skidding stop in front of the diner. It's still running when Gabriel jumps out of the driver's side and runs for the door, plowing through it. A few heads turn—truckers and other early-morning workers coming in for a plate of eggs and bacon before they start their long day. Gabriel finds me in my booth by the window quickly enough, exactly where I told him I'd be waiting.

A mix of emotions—rage, relief, horror—flashes across his handsome face as charges toward me. "Mercy." All he says is my name as he falls into the booth seat, curling his palm around my nape, his forehead falling against mine. The bags under his eyes are dark, like he hasn't slept in days. His clothes—normally fresh and well-fitting—are rumpled as if picked off the floor and thrown on, his hair tousled, likely from countless finger strokes. It brings me an odd sense of reassurance to see him so disheveled, that both Bane and Vic were wrong about him, and that I was right.

Gabriel has another side to him, even if none of them have seen it.

But that tiny voice in the back of my head can't stop asking what side they've seen that I haven't. Is it the side that hires men like Bane to capture wives of their enemies?

I can't dwell on that right now. If I do, I'll break.

I inhale the delicious scent of soap and cologne. "I'm a mess. I need a shower," I whisper, and it comes out sounding like an apology. The last one I had was in our Vegas hotel room, back when I didn't *really* understand what it meant to be dating Gabriel Easton, when I didn't truly comprehend the danger, beyond threats from an FBI agent. Now I'm wearing layers of dried sweat and dust and blood, poorly masked by a murdered woman's clothing.

"You'll get one as soon as we get you home." His thumb strokes the cut in my lip, his concerned gaze leveling on what I confirmed in the restroom mirror is an impressive bruise across my cheekbone. I've earned plenty of stares since I stepped through the diner's door. At one point, the night waitress offered to call the police for me. I begged her not to, told her she'd only make things worse if she did.

He curls a hand around mine, testing the dark purple ring around my wrists where the handcuffs dug into my flesh with the gentlest touch. The muscle in his jaw ticks before the curse slips out. "If he weren't already dead, I'd go out there and kill him myself."

"It's nothing that won't heal." I say that as much for my own comfort as his. "Are you going to try and find his place?" I told him about Bane's little desert homestead—and all the trophies I discovered during my escape—on his drive here.

"They're on their way there now."

I have no idea who "they" is—probably some of Farley's guys. "I don't know if the directions I gave you are any good." I only made three turns and I wrote them down on the scrap with Gabriel's number, along with approximate minutes driving, in case I did find myself at the edge of a cliff and needed to backtrack.

"Don't worry, they'll find it." He sounds so sure.

"And they'll clean up?"

He pulls back a touch, his steady eyes meeting mine. "They'll clean everything up so there are no questions, no police, no need for explanation. They'll make it like you were never there."

Make it like I didn't kill a man.

I nod. Oddly enough, I don't feel guilt for killing Bane. It was in self defense, and he deserved it a hundred times over based on the evidence that tumbled out with me when I fell through the ceiling. Still, I can't seem to shake the *click-click-click* sound of the gun chamber as I pulled the trigger and nothing fired.

But, as I sat here, waiting for Gabriel to arrive, feeling all the pitiful glances cast my way, I realized that I can never explain what happened. Because to answer any questions would open doors that need to remain shut—about Gabriel, about our relationship, about my father.

In this life, there is no room for answers to questions that shouldn't be asked.

I get that now.

"Where's Bane's phone?" Gabriel asks.

"Here. Plugged in." I fish it out from the corner of the booth. "How long before your father calls it, do you think?" Gabriel was adamant that I not answer any call that comes through.

"I don't know. Hours? Days? I don't even know if this is the phone Bane was using for calls with my father. But the longer he thinks Bane is alive and holding you, the better. At least until we get your father better protected. I'm working on getting my guy Chops switched to his cell but it's not easy, not with my father in the mix."

"Otherwise, Vlad will try to use him to get to you," I say, my voice hollow.

"God, Mercy, I'm so sorry." Shame morphs his features. "This is my fault."

I can't bring myself to ease his conscience by telling him it's not. I'm no fool. If not for Gabriel's help, my father would surely be dead by now. But it *is* Gabriel's fault that he tracked me down in the parking lot that day and made me a twisted and depraved offer I couldn't refuse. He knew who he is and what world he was dragging me into.

But he never hid that, and I fell for him anyway. That fault sits entirely on my shoulders. Still, despite everything that's happened, all I feel now is joy and solace that I'm in his arms again. I can't imagine being anywhere else.

"I've never been more scared than I have been these past two days," he admits, swallowing hard. "That you were gone was bad enough. That you were with that psychopath...." His teeth grit.

Gabriel knew exactly what kind of man Bane was.

But of course he did. Vic's words linger in the back of my mind. "The things Bane did to your cousin—"

"Shhh… I know." His lip graze mine, tentative over the cut. "It's over though. No one's going to hurt you again."

"No, that's not where I was going with that." I find his chest with my palm, pressing against it to push him back a touch, enough that I can meet his gaze and judge the truth of his answer. I wasn't going to bring this up but I can't help it. "Did you ever hire Bane to do anything for you? Did you ever ask him to do *those kinds of things* to anyone—"

"*No*. He was my father's dog. He did what my father wanted. We stayed far away from him. I'd only ever met him once, and that was enough."

"And all those people…" All those bones. "Was that all just for your father? Or was it for the family?" Did Bane ever torture people to help Gabriel and Caleb?

"I can't control what my father does, Mercy. That should be obvious by now."

"But you told him what your uncle did. How your uncle was the one who helped put Vlad in jail. You knew he'd send Bane after them and you knew what Bane would do. To your family."

Gabriel hesitates, but then nods. "We made a deal with Merrick and Vince to help take care of each other's problems. But it's gotten messy, and it isn't unfolding exactly as we'd hoped. There are a lot of pieces in play that I can't explain right here, but it all begins and ends with our father. I'm not proud of any of this, but I don't want this life. You know that, Mercy."

"I thought I did."

"You *do*," he pushes, as if using a stern voice to push out any lingering doubt. "And there's only one way Caleb and I can avoid it." He looks meaningfully at me.

Vlad Easton has to die.

"A top-up?" The night waitress hovers by the table with a full pot of coffee, a ketchup stain on her blue diner uniform, her suspicious gaze on Gabriel. I'll bet she thinks he's behind all my bumps and bruises. The few patrons at the counter seem to be thinking the same thing, based on their judgmental looks. It's probably best we get out of here before one of them decides to challenge Gabriel.

"No, I'm fine," I answer with what I hope is an appreciative smile. The cup she poured me earlier is still full and now cold, sitting next to an untouched plate of toast and eggs. I push the wad of cash toward her. "I think that should cover everything." I can't keep Bane's blood money and, with luck, that will buy her silence.

Her eyes widen at the bundle, but then, with a curt nod, she collects it. "Have yourself a better day today." With another cagey glance at Gabriel, she strolls back behind the counter, tucking her windfall into her apron pocket.

Gabriel curls his arm around my shoulders and leads me from the diner and into the back of the SUV, sliding in beside me. Farley sits in the driver seat. At some point, the enormous bodyguard climbed into the spot without my notice. Now he meets my eyes in the rear-view mirror. "Glad to have you back." A rare smile touches his lips.

"It's a long drive. Here, take this and you'll wake up in Phoenix." Gabriel produces a small blue pill from a container along with a bottle of water.

"What is it?" Somewhere in my distant memory, I recall a humiliating experience with doctor-prescribed sleeping pill that I don't want to relive, especially not with Farley present.

The corner of Gabriel's mouth curls. "Not Ambien. You should be fine. And if you're not, I'll wake you up."

I hesitate for another second before downing the pill.

Gabriel ropes his arm around me and pulls the uninjured side of my face into the crook of his neck. He seems unwilling to release me. "Drive us home," he orders.

Home. That word brings one place to mind and it's not my apartment. It's the palatial house atop the mountain. It's the lap pool overlooking the city lights. It's Gabriel's bed, the sheets silky soft and cool. And safe.

But is anywhere truly safe anymore?

I don't have much time to dwell on that thought. Within minutes, a soothing wave of relaxation is sinking deep into my limbs. I fall asleep with my head against Gabriel's chest, memorizing his strong and steady heartbeat.

I'M groggy when we step into the house, the sleeping pill effective in knocking me out for the full trip back. It takes me a moment to register the yappy chihuahua that greets me. "Whose dog is this?"

"Long story," is all Gabriel manages to say before Michelle charges forward.

"Mercy! Thank God you're okay!" She's about four feet away when she falters, as if only then remembering how badly she betrayed me.

Moe trails behind her, a quiet shadow who used to leave me unsettled. Next to Bane though, he's as huggable as a child's plush teddy bear. I was relieved when Gabriel confirmed that he had survived Bane's attack with nothing more than a flesh wound. I would have felt guilty had he lost his life trying to protect me. I was also glad to learn that Michelle helped Moe by stemming the blood flow and getting Farley there, rather than running and screaming out the door as fast as she could.

With a hard swallow, Michelle says, "We were all so worried about you."

The animosity and hurt that absorbed me the night I found out my best friend was working with the FBI has evaporated. It may return once this surreal fog that shrouds my new reality—postcaptivity—lifts, but for now I'm happy to see her. I offer her a small smile.

She returns it, though her brow furrows as she takes inventory of the dark purple rings around my wrists. I know she's wondering how I earned those. Her lips even part as if to ask, but then she hesitates. "I drew a bath for you in Gabriel's room. It just finished. It's still nice and hot."

"In *our* room," Gabriel corrects, smoothing a palm over my back. I haven't been beyond his reach since he settled into the booth at the diner.

"Right. Of course." She fumbles over her words. "And there are burgers and salads laid out on the counter. Or I can make you a sandwich, some scrambled eggs? Some fruit, too, if that's what you feel like…." Her words drift as Caleb saunters over. She watches him like a cautious animal after having been kicked.

"I will admit, the traitor's been the perfect little helper around here, especially with all the extra bodies to feed." He offers her a disapproving look that counters his praise before shifting his attention to me. The black eye that he came home with that night of the explosion is healing, hints of green where purple used to blemish his skin. "So the beast was killed by the beauty. Can't wait to hear the full story."

"I'm in no rush to tell it."

"No, I guess not." Caleb's fingertip grazes my mottled cheek, a deep scowl marring his normally unbothered expression. "We'll make Vlad pay for this; we promise."

Right now, all I want to do is hide and not have to face anyone. Certainly not start conversations about revenge.

A child's laughter pulls my attention to the terrace beyond the living room. It's mid-afternoon and there is a naked child climbing into the pool, followed closely by a young dark-haired woman. I frown. "Is that *my* red bikini?"

"Like I said, there's *a lot* going on that I need to explain." Gabriel sighs heavily. His hands curl around my waist and he gently guides me toward his wing.

"So, that's Puff's girlfriend, son, and mother by the pool." Warm water sluices across my scalp, followed by Gabriel's fingers, gently working the shampoo suds from my hair. "And Puff is the leader of the gang who mules your drugs."

"Right. And he's currently serving time in Fulcort. You might have seen him when you were there to visit your dad. He has a large tattoo of a dragon on his face."

I do remember seeing that guy once. According to my father's cellmate, Crazy Bob, he was high up in the gang food chain. A young woman was there to see him, maybe the same one who's now being fed three square meals and top-shelf tequila to mask the fact that Gabriel and Caleb are holding her and her family against their will.

"Puff the Magic Dragon," I murmur, piecing things together. "I thought he was supposed to be friendly."

Gabriel flashes a wry smile. "Yeah, well, the Fulcort version, not so much. Especially not after this. I tried to explain that it was either we do it this way and hide them here, or my father loses patience with us and sends men to get them. Or worse, Bane. At least this way they're safe until Vlad is dealt with, once and for all." Gabriel caps the shampoo and reaches for the conditioner. He's been tending to me as a nurse cares for a patient—removing my clothes with clinical hands, lifting me into the deep soaker tub, settling onto the edge where he can delicately wash my body. Even now, mostly clean, I haven't caught his dark blue eyes wandering over my nakedness once. Normally, he can't keep his eyes and hands to himself.

He's about as far from the Gabriel Easton I first met that day in the parking lot as he can get, when he thought a blow job in exchange for saving my father's life was an acceptable launching point for negotiation.

What's even more shockingly different is how he's divulging the inner workings of his and Caleb's scheming to me without hesitation.

"So you're basically saying those women and that child are going through all this because of me."

"You can't think like that, Mercy—"

"But it's true."

"No, it's not. This is all on Vlad. Everything. I'm just trying to mitigate the damage he can cause." There's a sharpness in his tone, and his jaw is tense.

"You hate that you had to do it, don't you?"

After a moment, he admits, "It made me sick. But we didn't have a choice. If I didn't do this, Bane would have hurt you. After he went for them."

I shudder at the thought of Bane with that little boy in his van. I'm not going to pretend to agree with his rationalization, or condone it, but I need to trust that what Gabriel's doing was the best option for these people. "They've been treated well, at least?" Not locked up in a windowless room and slapped around?

"They've got everything they could possibly want and need while they wait this out. No one's laid a hand on them," Gabriel confirms. "Even when Puff's mother stabbed Moe in the forearm with her crochet needle, no one so much as raised a finger." He shakes his head. "She looks so sweet and innocent. No one expected it."

The genuine perplexity in his face sparks a bubble of laughter inside me. It escapes in a deep cackle that I can't seem to dull once it starts. "Poor Moe. He keeps getting the short end of the stick. Or should I say needle."

Gabriel's eyes linger on me.

"What?"

"Nothing, it's nice to hear you laugh. I wasn't sure if I'd ever hear it again after what you've been through." He glowers at the dark bruising around my wrist. "How long did Bane leave you hanging there?"

"I'm not sure," I admit. "It was a while." My muscles still ache from the strain. Tomorrow will likely be worse. But I'd rather think about anything other than my ordeal. "So now what?"

"Now we hide you as long as we can and figure out a way to deal with Vlad. He's well protected in there."

"You mean kill him, don't you?" I ask softly. Vic was right about that much; they do have a plan.

He weaves his fingers through mine, studying our joined hands quietly for a moment. "It's not something I ever imaged myself being a part of, but we don't have a choice. He'd burn the whole damn world down if it means winning. Getting rid of him is the *only* way you'll ever be truly safe. And when that problem is dealt with, we can release Puff's family and be done with this world once and for all. Start a new chapter, you and me. Live a normal life."

His promise sounds nice.

But can life with Gabriel *ever* be normal?

Or will it simply be different degrees of shadiness?

How do you shed the identity of a notorious crime family? Will Caleb and Gabriel be satisfied with doing business legally? Will they accept that they can't just get everything they want, how they wanted? It's all they've ever known.

I can't believe we're talking about killing someone. Not just someone… Vlad Easton. I think back to all those bones that belonged to all those people Vlad had Bane kill. And he knew what Bane was, what he was capable of. They *all* knew. "Realistically, how long before he knows I've escaped?"

Gabriel purses his lips. "Hard to say. Now that my uncle is out of the picture and he thinks we're obeying him, Vlad has no reason to call Bane for the foreseeable future. He's using other guys to deal with the cartel. But the real issue is that damn agent, Lewis. She's been by a few times. She thinks I found out you two were talking and killed you. She's banking on bringing me in for your murder."

"She's determined to arrest you any way she can."

"Yeah. And she's been by to talk to your boss."

I curse under my breath. Martha has stood by me through the entire case with my father. I don't know if she—the director of a drug rehab center—will be as sympathetic if she finds out I'm in love with the son of a criminal overlord, known for ties to the drug world.

"And when she checks in again with Mary's Way tomorrow morning and your boss says you've called in sick, because you *are* calling in sick"—he caps that off with a glare that warns me to not challenge him—"she'll come straight here. If I don't produce you, she'll arrest me and likely storm in with a warrant. If I do produce you, my dad will likely hear about it through his contacts. And if that happens…."

"He'll go after my father."

"He's the likeliest next target, especially now that my father doesn't have Bane at his disposal."

"So, basically you're saying we have until tomorrow and then every minute beyond that is sheer luck."

"I'm not going to let anything happen to him. Or to you. Ever again." He brings one wrist to his mouth, his lips feather-soft against the welts. "It's like you were made just for me," he murmurs more to himself.

"Really? This was my calling? Do I need to remind you how we met? You're a scoundrel and a criminal," I say dryly, but cap it off with a mischievous smirk.

He reaches out to brush a wet strand of hair off my forehead. "But you're here to turn me into a decent man."

"I have my work cut out for me then." A tiny spark ignites in my stomach. After the ordeal I've been through, this playfulness is nice, familiar.

Gabriel collects the sponge and smooths it over my neck and collarbone again, though he's already washed there. He continues on, tracing the swell of my breasts. I see a glimmer of interest, but he doesn't take it further.

"You know I won't break, right? You *can* touch me."

He inhales deeply, and lets his fingertips slip down to graze my skin. It's a fleeting move though, before he pulls back. "I know that's how this all started, but we're more than that."

"We are." I reach out to collect his hand in mine, bringing it to my lips.

He watches the move. "You, gone for these few days… me, not knowing if I'd ever see you again? Not knowing if you'd want anything to do with me if I did get you back? I can't live without you, Mercy. I know that without a shadow of a doubt, and I don't ever want to try." He hesitates, a rare nervous look dancing over his face. "I want you to—"

A knuckle raps on the door a moment before Caleb pokes his head in, interrupting Gabriel midsentence. "How's our sexy little killer doing?"

Some things never change. I sink lower in the tub to ensure the pervert can't catch a glimpse. "I'm fine. Thanks for asking. Now get out."

"Ouch. Came back from the desert with a little extra salt, huh?"

"Better listen to her. She'll pull the trigger," Gabriel warns, his eyes never leaving mine.

"But I come bearing gifts." Caleb waves a first aid kit before tossing it onto the nearby counter. "There's some ibuprofen in there, but if you want the good stuff, say the word." He winks at me.

"Advil's fine, thank you." At least Caleb's being considerate—a rare occasion. Though, he's offering me heavy narcotics.

Gabriel jerks his head toward his brother. "Come on, get the fuck out. You're interrupting."

"Nothing good, from the looks of it." Caleb's phone

rings. "Oh look. It's the club calling *my* number again, because you've decided to stop answering your phone for the day."

Gabriel smirks. "They must think you have something to do with running it."

"I don't know why they'd think that," Caleb mutters and, instead of leaving to answer the call like any decent human would, he answers it right there. "Gabriel Easton's answering service. What's up, Mike? Let me guess, the booze truck is late."

But it isn't the club manager whose voice carries over the receiver. It's a female and she's hysterical.

"Whoa, Ryley, *slow down*." Caleb pauses to listen, his brow furrowing. Whatever he catches in her frenzied rambling causes the color to drain from his tanned face. "*When*?"

Gabriel, sensing an issue, shifts his attention to his brother. "What's goin' on?"

But Caleb doesn't acknowledge the question, his expression turning grimmer by the second. Abruptly, he says, "I'm on my way," and ends the call.

"What is it?" Gabriel's shoulders are tense. It's clear this is far beyond anything to do with liquor deliveries.

Caleb's mouth opens and closes several times, as if unable to find the right words. When he speaks, his voice is gruff and hollow. "Ryley went in early to meet the delivery truck and found Mike in our office. Doesn't look like he ever left last night."

"Mike. *Our* Mike." Gabriel looks like he's been punched across the face.

"There were two other guys there. She didn't recognize them."

"When you say *found*…." I let my words trail, my stomach sinking as the true gravity of his words settle in.

More victims, more dead bodies.

With a rage-filled roar, Caleb throws his phone across the bathroom.

FIFTEEN
GABRIEL

Voices buzz over radios and in conversation. Empire must be hosting half the Phoenix police department this afternoon, with every uniform from beat cops to forensic lab rats to this soft-bellied detective in a golf shift and tan pants, leaning against my bar.

"Are we almost done here?"

Detective Huxley pauses scrawling across his notepad to offer me a flat look. "You got somewhere more important to be?"

"Yeah." I don't bother denying it. Home with Mercy. The last thing I wanted to do was leave her and come down here, but if I didn't, the cops would be on my doorstep within hours to question me. There's a guard on every access point to our property and house, but it doesn't matter. A thousand of Farley's men guarding Mercy wouldn't bring me comfort.

"Three dead bodies were found in your establishment. *No*, we're not *almost done here*. We haven't even begun." The detective snorts as he turns his attention back to his page, giving his bushy mustache a twitch with his fingers. "And before you ask, *no*, you won't be opening your club tonight, or any other day this week. Maybe not even this month."

"Can we at least go in to collect a few—"

"Nope. Your office is a crime scene, and we can't risk contaminating it any more than it was when your bar manager went in there." His smile is toothy and fake. "Now, the sooner you cooperate with the investigation, the sooner we might be able to get out of your hair."

"And how exactly are we not cooperating, detective?" Caleb sidles up beside me, his arms folded across his chest. I guess his attempt to woo the female officer into letting us upstairs didn't go as planned. "We've given you guys access codes to the security cameras; we've answered *all* your questions. What more do you want?"

"All of them, huh?" The detective snorts. "You really think this is a robbery gone bad?"

"Well, I don't know. Is the safe cracked?" Caleb retorts.

"Nah. Untouched."

"Then I guess not, *detective*."

I fight the urge to elbow my brother. Hostility will not help us here. But I know he's only lashing out to hide the fact that he's devastated. Mike may have been our club manager, but he was more than that—he was a friend.

Another dead friend because of our father.

Huxley scans his page. "Tell me about Jimmy Jones and Ivan Clark."

Fuck. So that's who the other two bodies were. From what Ryley told us through hysterical sobs, the men's faces wouldn't have been recognizable. The cops must have run fingerprints on the bodies to identify them. Both would show up quickly in the database.

"Don't know 'em," Caleb claims before I get a chance to speak.

I stifle my sigh. It would take even a mediocre detective an hour to poke holes in that claim. "We know *of* them. What do you want to know?"

"They didn't work for you?"

"*For us*? No. They both used to work for our father at his banquet halls." Before the feds shut them down. "Not sure what Ivan has been up to lately." Besides managing all the drug-running for the greater Phoenix area and being one of my father and Peter's most trusted men. "And last I heard, JJ was doing odd jobs." Like sneaking down to Mexico to burn down a cartel's drug operation warehouse in Hermosillo. That must be why Navarro targeted them. Or maybe they made themselves easy victims, though I'd be surprised. They've been in this game long enough. But maybe they would have benefited from one of Vlad Easton's lessons on watching their backs.

"So, they were a part of the family business, is what you're saying." A knowing gleam shines in the detective's eyes. Of course he knows who JJ and Ivan were. He was merely testing us.

Caleb flashes a toothy grin. "The Easton family is full of entrepreneurs. Not sure *which* business you're referring to, Detective *Huxley*. Sorry, I didn't catch your first name."

For fuck's sakes, Caleb. Now is not the time for intimidation tactics.

Huxley's jaw tenses as he and my brother lock gazes for one... two... three beats, before he shifts his attention to me. "How did JJ and Ivan know Mike Stoll?"

"No idea." They didn't. They'd never met. This was Navarro, sending a message to my father, a retaliatory move that says all Eastons are fair game and his reach can be just as damaging. Mike was a pillar at Empire and a major reason the club has done as well as it has. Business-wise, losing him is a major blow.

"So then, if he didn't know them and they didn't work here, what were those two doing in your club, after hours, with your club manager?" Huxley presses.

I shake my head. "Like I said, no idea. Wasn't anything to do with the club."

"Huxley!" someone calls out.

Huxley seeks out the voice. "Give me a minute, will ya? I'll be right back." He lumbers away.

"Dad wanted to start a war? He's got one," Caleb growls, just loud enough for me to hear. "I'm going to fucking kill him, and then we're going after Navarro."

My stomach tenses. That is exactly what can't happen. "And where does it end?"

"I don't give a shit."

"Well, *I do*." Because it's not just our lives on the line anymore, and this life that is starting to take shape in the recesses of my mind—still blurry except for one very clear image, or rather face—can't happen if we let ourselves get dragged deeper in.

"So, what the fuck are we supposed to do then? Bend over and take it up the ass? They fucking killed Mike, Gabe. *Mike*!"

"I know." It takes everything in me not to scream. But something has been pricking the back of my skull since that phone call from Ryley. Mike has been a pillar for Empire since day one. Any expansion plans we might have been toying with? We need Mike to succeed. It's as if Navarro knew exactly how to cripple our dreams.

If Bane weren't dead, I might wonder if our father was behind Mike's murder, as well. Another lesson, to keep our attention where he wants it. But Dad would never have Ivan and JJ killed, not unless they betrayed him. He needs them too much.

"Dad's going to hear about JJ and Ivan sooner rather than later and when he does, all hell will break loose." His precious world of Harriet is a complicated weave of runners and mules, layers of dealers, and between Uncle Peter's removal and now these two murdered, and the reluctance of Puff's crew, it just took a massive hit. Key players—the people who run shit and strike fear—are gone. Our territory, all of Easton's customers, is now prime picking for Navarro and that will infuriate Vlad. "God only knows what he'll do next, but it'll be something big…." And then around and around we go on this savage merry-go-round.

It also means he's likely to call Bane to do his dirty

work. But no one's answering that call. How long before he grows suspicious?

Caleb snorts. "Give him enough time and he might take Harriet out all on his own. It's already standing on three wobbly legs."

"We can't give him that time." Vlad Easton has nothing left to lose. I have *everything* left to lose. "It's time we put the rest of the plan in motion."

Caleb assesses our surroundings before confirming, "Now that Mercy's safe, Cali has carte blanche. I told them the sooner, the better."

So, Merrick and Vince have the go-ahead to tap whatever shoulders they can reach within Fulcort's walls. Good. "And I told Puff and Donny there would be zero reprisal if something were to happen." That's three major factions with a lot of influence, with open hunting licenses. The challenge is getting through his tight ring of protection, something our father is paying amply for. There is one way to fix that. "I'll pay George a little visit." Explain to our magician accountant that all those hidden pockets of money he's been managing for the Easton family will be better served in any way other than keeping Vlad alive. Then it's just a matter of spreading that message through the appropriate channels. If people hear the Vlad Easton Protection Fund has dried up, they won't be so eager to stick their necks on the line.

"Gladly. As soon as we can get out of here."

I hesitate. "And we're going to have a sit-down with Navarro."

Caleb's jaw drops, not expecting that minor revision. "Are you fucking insane?"

"Maybe." The last thing I want to do is get in a room with people who castrate and behead their competition, especially after our father just burned down one of their warehouse operations. "We don't have a choice. We need to get ahead of this before Dad retaliates and make a deal. I'm putting a call in to the Operator." A guy who connects people who need connecting. His veins may as well be synced to the dark web because there doesn't seem to be a single contact number he can't find. Sure, we could track down Navarro's minions and play pass-the-message until it reaches Navarro's ears, probably around the same time word reaches our father's ears that his sons are trying to meet with the cartel behind his back. The Operator is the fastest and most discrete way to do this.

"No," Caleb says with grim resolution. "I don't trust them. No *fucking* way, Gabe."

"Then you don't have to come with me."

"Boy, all those news crews outside. Lots of PR for your club, gentlemen, though I'm guessing it's not the kind you want," that familiar, arrogant voice calls out, interrupting what would have turned into a heated conversation, one we have no business having here.

I turn to find Special Agent Lewis prowling toward us. Caleb gapes at me for another moment before snapping his attention to her and shifting gears. "Three times in three nights. Gosh, Kennedy, I haven't felt this special in *so* long."

"And you have three more bodies to add to your collection."

I can hear Caleb's molars grinding beside me. "One of them was a *good* friend."

"It looks like being friends with you two requires hazard pay."

I take a step forward to plant myself firmly between them before Caleb snaps and makes this night ten times worse. "What are you doing here? This seems like a Phoenix PD thing."

She surveys the room. "When two of the deceased are known high-ranking members of organized crime and the cause is clearly homicide, it becomes more than a Phoenix PD *thing*."

Great. News of Ivan and JJ is already circulating, which means Dad will know soon enough. The bastard will have the nerve to be outraged by something a halfwit could have seen coming from a thousand miles away.

"Well, whoever they are, if you could help move this investigation along so we can get our club up and running, it would be much appreciated. We can't afford to take this financial hit."

"Anything for you fine, upstanding businessmen." Lewis offers a wide smile but it falls off quickly. Turning to me, she asks, "Have you heard from Mercy Wheeler yet? I still haven't been able to reach her."

"Yeah, actually. She said she was out of town visiting a friend. Near Sedona, I think. Terrible reception. She called her boss to take next week off. The woman's been working so hard up until now, she deserves it. Should be back in a few days."

Lewis's lips twist with open disdain.

I could have told the truth, for my sake, but it's better I don't—for the sake of Mercy's father. If I have Lewis pegged right, she'll be calling Mercy's boss tomorrow morning at 9:00 a.m. sharp and asking to listen to the voicemail. If she checks the cell towers, she'll know Mercy's in Phoenix. But that's tomorrow and a lot can change between now and then.

Which reminds me, I need to call Donny again and bust his balls about getting Chops moved.

Huxley returns. "You have a hardwired hidden camera in your office that's not part of your overall security system."

It was only a matter of time before they found that. "No, it's not. It's a private camera."

"Where does it feed to?" His eyebrows arch in question.

"A hard drive. Caleb or I turn it on when we need it, and we weren't here last night to turn it on."

"Of course not. That would be too convenient," Huxley mutters, shaking his head. "We'll still need to take a look at that hard drive."

"Knock yourself out, though there won't be anything on it." The last time I turned that camera on was when Merrick and Vince made contact for the first time to hatch our dual escape plan. It got wiped clean after that.

"Umm… actually, there *might* be something on there." Caleb scratches his chin in mock-thought.

"Make sure you have a clear view, Agent Lewis. I think you'll find it *highly* educational."

I don't have to ask what they're going to find on there. Caleb loves to record himself fucking. Normally I'd be struggling not to laugh but my mood is dour. "If there's nothing else?"

"For now." Huxley waves us away.

"I'll be seeing you soon," Agent Lewis hollers after us.

"Hopefully after you watch that footage," Caleb throws back with a wink.

SIXTEEN
MERCY

I CLOSE my eyes and inhale the delicious scent of coconut lingering on my skin. The afternoon sun is scalding, and yet I can't bring myself to hide inside, and so I remain out here on our private terrace, cooling off in the lap pool, slathering myself with sunscreen, and trying to ignore Farley's men watching me.

At least I'm not the only one who's occupying their attention. Down below on the main terrace, Puff's mother hides beneath the shade of an umbrella, crocheting baby booties. Puff's girlfriend and son haven't left the pool in hours, the little boy has shifted between maniacal giggling to hysterical temper tantrums several times over. He's currently working through the latter.

"Someone's not happy."

I jump at the sound of Gabriel's voice, my heart instantly racing. *I'm fine, I'm safe*, I remind myself, pressing a palm against my chest. "He just needs a nap."

"He's not the only one."

Gabriel *does* look exhausted, the bags under his eyes darker than they were this morning.

He closes the distance, his steps slow, his posture sunken as if carrying a heavy weight. The second I'm within reach, he doesn't hesitate to slip his arms around my waist and pull me to him. "I'm sorry. I didn't mean to scare you."

I sigh at the feel of Gabriel's lips against my neck. "It's okay. I just seem to startle more easily now." A door slam, a shout, a knock… everything puts me on edge. I tell myself that it won't always be this way, that I was able to shed what happened to me after Fleet, but is that even true? A lot of the women who come into Mary's have been carrying the darkness of a traumatic experience for years, sometimes buried so deep they don't realize it's a driving force for everything that's amiss in their lives.

"You taste like sunscreen," Gabriel whispers in my ear. "And you're tense. Try and relax. *Please.*"

I take a deep breath and sink back against his chest. And remind myself that Gabriel is safe. He will do anything to keep me protected—even if it means doing things that will turn his own stomach.

I'm not the only one who's tense. Gabriel's body, normally a hard expanse of muscle, is far more rigid than usual.

"Did Mike have family?"

"Yeah. His parents and sister, a few nephews. They live in Vegas. We'll have to make a trip out there to pay our respects in person."

"Of course," I hear myself say, though I'm in no

rush to go back to Nevada ever again. "How bad was it at Empire?"

"Bad." It's a moment before he elaborates. "They wouldn't let us into the office so we didn't actually see Mike, but from what Ryley described.... We can get the coroner's report if we want to. I don't know if I want to."

I only met their club manager once and yet fear spasms inside me. "Was this another lesson from your father?" Did his goons make Mike scream like Bane made his victims scream?

"No. This was retaliation for something my father did."

I hesitate. "What did he do?"

"Started a full-out war with the cartel. A man named Luiz Navarro."

My stomach twists. Agent Lewis said the cartel was moving in, that there were murders, that Gabriel was getting in over his head. She warned that he'd get himself killed. "A turf war?"

"Basically. Dad wants to take over Perri's territory now that Caleb has cleared a path and make Navarro think twice about trying to step in on either." Gabriel sighs. "Now Caleb and I and Empire are getting dragged into it. I guess it was only a matter of time before that happened. I mean, everyone knows we own the club. That makes the place a target."

I'm about to push for more information, but commotion down below breaks my focus. Caleb and several of Farley's men have surrounded the woman—Sasha, I've learned is her name. Caleb must have said something to infuriate her because she's rattling off a string of angry words in Spanish, so fast that I only manage to decipher a few curses. Her little boy, hugging her leg, begins to wail.

"What's going on?" I ask warily.

Gabriel shakes his head. "Caleb was right, it was stupid to bring them to our house. It's too risky, with Mike's murder and Lewis hovering. It's only a matter of time before the cops show up here and it won't matter how well we've treated them. We have to move them."

That's right. They're hostages here. Well-fed hostages sleeping in their own suites, but hostages nonetheless. "Where are you going to take them?"

"Santa Barbara. Merrick has a place there that they can hole up in for awhile."

Mention of a Perri reminds me of the last night I spent in Vegas. "You guys have gotten close."

"It's a means to an end. That's all."

I'm not sure if I believe that but I don't prod.

We watch as Caleb reaches for Sasha, hand out, palm up.

She slaps it away with another string of profanity, earning Gabriel's snort.

"She doesn't seem like she wants to go anywhere."

"She thinks we're escorting her out to a desert cliff."

I survey the terrace. The poor woman and her child are surrounded by a ring of intimidating men with guns, the very same ones who dragged her out of her house. "I don't blame her. They're all guys like Bane as far as she's concerned."

Gabriel frowns as he takes in the scene again, as if

through new eyes. "Give her some breathing room!" he hollers, pulling Caleb's attention up to us. "And let her talk to Puff."

Caleb juts his chin in acknowledgement and digs out his phone. Farley's men shift away, though none too close to the old woman sitting in the shade with her crochet needles.

Gabriel sighs heavily against my nape, sending a shiver down my spine. "I'm so tired. I can't remember the last time I slept."

"You didn't sleep on the way back from Nevada?"

"No. I watched *you* sleep." His voice carries amusement "And drool."

An unexpected laugh bursts out of me. "I was not drooling."

"You were. You had a little bit of it running down right here." His index finger drags along the corner of my mouth.

I swat his hand away, but then collect it in mine and tug him wordlessly back into the house, hitting the automated switch for the blinds. In seconds, the bedroom is cast into shadows.

He smirks. "Why do I feel like I'm being put to bed?"

"Because you are. Come on, arms up. I know how you like to sleep," I tease.

He obeys, and I peel his T-shirt up over his head, revealing a canvas of smooth, taut muscle and warm skin. A familiar rush stirs in my lower belly as I unfasten his belt and his jeans, and work them down his powerful thighs.

But that lust is competing with something more potent—something gnawing in my chest, this desperate need to wrap my arms around him, to protect him from whatever danger his father is stirring up for him.

For us.

For our future.

I can't live in a world where Gabriel Easton doesn't exist.

He kicks his jeans away and then tugs at the strings of my damp bikini without any preamble. The skimpy black material tumbles to the floor, leaving me standing before him, aching for his warm hands, his capable touch. But instead of hungry eyes over my naked body, a tortured gaze measures my injuries.

"I'll heal," I remind him. Already, the cut on my lip isn't so angry, the welts that accompany the bruising on my wrists have shrunk, my cheek doesn't throb.

"I know," he whispers, lifting my knuckles to his mouth. But it's a chaste kiss that ends quickly, and then he's pulling the sheets back and guiding me into bed. He slips in behind me, my body fitting into a perfect spoon with his, his arm sliding beneath my head. I hear the deep inhale and I smile. He does that every time he comes up behind me—burrows his face into my hair. He's always loved the scent of my shampoo.

Instinctively, I roll my hips into his pelvis. I don't think I've ever seen Gabriel naked and *not* erect, and yet he remains flaccid against me.

"I just need to hold you right now, babe," he whispers, his arms tightening. "Hold you and not think about all the shit I'm gonna have to wade through to get us out of this mess."

"Of course." I reach back blindly and stroke my fingers through his sable-brown hair. My heart pangs for him. He's lost three good friends in the last week, I don't know what's happening with the cartel, though it can't be good, and then there's the issue of his father. No matter how hateful—how evil—the prick is, giving the order to have him killed must weigh on Gabriel's conscience.

"I agree with you by the way," I hear myself say. I've thought about it all afternoon, and Gabriel's right.

"About what?" His voice is throaty.

"Life imprisonment hasn't stopped your father, and too many people have died because of him." The few that I know of are already too many. Gabriel's aunt's screams, her pleas for her life, still ring in my ear. Surely her mistake in falling in love with his uncle didn't earn her a bullet. The guiltless flight crew, and even Finn and Felix, whose playboy lifestyle didn't warrant their end either. Mike had nothing to do with any of this. And my poor father… I won't let anything happen to him while he's trapped in that hellhole. "Too many people will die if someone doesn't stop him. *You* have to stop him."

A long stretch of silence meets my words.

"Gabriel?" I roll over, to find him with a pensive look on his face. "What are you thinking about?" I remember a time when I didn't care to ask that question, I didn't want to know what went on in his devious mind.

"I'm thinking about how I never imagined being

with a woman could feel like this." He reaches up to push the strands of hair off my face. "You know I'm in love with you, right?"

Flutters stir in my stomach as I press my forehead against his. "I remember." But it's nice to hear him say it again, without my frenzied prompting.

"Okay. Good." He closes his eyes. "You want to know something else?"

"Yeah?"

It's a moment before he speaks. "I'm terrified." His angular jaw tenses. "People I care about could get hurt. You, Caleb, my Empire staff. Too many things could go wrong, I feel like a fist is tightening around us, and I'm fucking *terrified*." It comes out as a whisper, as if he's afraid to admit the words.

Gabriel Easton, the cocky, dominant, stubborn rogue who says and does what he wants, when he wants, who walks around as if he owns the entire world and the world owes him everything, has never shown a hint of vulnerability. Now, it bleeds from his voice.

And that scares the shit out of me.

But he doesn't need to hear that. He needs to hear that everything will be fine.

I push my fingers through his hair in gentle, soothing strokes. "It's okay to be scared."

"No, it's not. There's no room for fear in what we're trying to do here. It'll cloud our thoughts and get us killed."

"Fine. Then let yourself be terrified right here, right now, with me. And then when you get up and go out there, you pack it away and you do what you need to do." I smooth my hand over his chest, reveling in his body heat. "As long as you don't do *anything* stupid, no matter what. Deal?"

"Deal." His eyes are still closed but he's smiling. "How did I get so lucky?" he murmurs drowsily.

"Because you propositioned the right girl in the prison parking lot."

He answers with a weak snort.

My fingers itch to slip down and stroke him to life, just so I can feel him sinking into me again, and perhaps take his fear away for a short time. But he's exhausted, and so I stay my hand and enjoy the sound of his deepening breaths.

In minutes, he's fast asleep.

THE MICHELLE I KNEW—THE feisty, effervescent blond who laughed boldly and often—has been replaced by this twitchy version standing at the front door with her suitcase on one side and Moe on the other, her tired emerald-green eyes jumping with every movement.

"So, I guess this is goodbye?"

"Yeah, I guess so." I hesitate. "It's for the best." While I'm with Gabriel, I can never trust her.

She nods. "I understand." Her gaze darts to the far side of the living room, where Caleb and Gabriel are occupied in an intense conversation. Between the two of them, they've taken at least a dozen calls since Caleb pounded on our bedroom door to wake Gabriel.

The house is quiet again, with no screaming

toddlers, cursing girlfriends, or stabbing mothers. Our "guests" were escorted to a helicopter launchpad while Gabriel napped and flown to Merrick's coastal retreat for safekeeping. Apparently, Puff's little boy was completely enthralled.

Now it's just us, a small army of security, and a world full of uncertainty.

"Please tell them thank you...." She falters. "For letting me go home."

For letting her live, she means. Neither Gabriel nor Caleb had any intention of holding—or harming—Michelle, but Caleb was effective in his scare tactics and I'm not about to enlighten her. Besides, after our plane explosion and the triple homicide she witnessed in Vegas, I doubt she'd believe me. It's best she stays frightened—for her sake and Gabriel's. "You know Lewis will contact you again."

"Which is why I have a houseguest for the next little while." Her nervous eyes flip to Moe. "Hey roomie."

He answers her with a stony stare. What must he think about this babysitting assignment? Gabriel said they've given it to him while he's a lame duck from his injuries, but I remember him also saying Moe preferred protecting women and children, so maybe he's okay with being glued to her side.

"Just remember what you need to say." Caleb gave her the script and reinforced that she is not to veer from it.

"Speak no evil, hear no evil, see no evil." She chuckles weakly. "Yes, I know. Partying and gambling and drinking. *Lots* of drinking, so much that I blacked out and don't remember a thing, but Moe and I have fallen in love and Caleb, who? Honestly, Mercy, I don't want *any* part of whatever Lewis is trying to accomplish. I regret ever letting her talk me into it."

"You were trying to help your father. I can appreciate that." Of *all people*, I can empathize. But I can't forgive.

"For what it's worth, I *really* did think I was helping you with your father. I just didn't realize how you felt about Gabriel until it was too late." She reaches for her suitcase and steals another quick, wary glance Caleb's way. "We better go."

The urge to protect Gabriel from Agent Lewis is overwhelming. "If you talk, they *will* hear about it," I warn, mustering certainty in my voice as I take a step back. "Take care of yourself."

She hesitates but then darts forward, throwing her arms around me, whispering, "I hope you know what you're doing, Mercy."

It's a moment before I return the hug. "Don't worry. With all these guards around? Nothing's going to happen to me."

She pulls back, to meet my gaze. "Something *already* did."

Yes, a psychopath kidnapped me from under their noses. But that psychopath is dead. *I* killed him.

I take a deep, calming breath. "I'll be fine."

Her jaw tenses as if she wants to say more but decides against it. Diving in for one last tight squeeze, she breaks away abruptly. A teary gloss coats her eyes.

"Thank you, fine sir," she jokes as Moe collects her suitcase.

He grits his teeth at the strain in his forearm, the only sign that the crochet attack wound hurts.

With a chin-nod my way from Moe, they're gone, down the walkway, past the armed man standing next to the chartreuse wall of organ pipe cacti.

My best friend and confidant for years, who has stood by me through this ongoing nightmare with my father, is gone from my life. My first relationship casualty after choosing Gabriel.

But she chose someone else, too. I can understand why, and oddly enough it no longer stings. Maybe it's because of what I've been through.

But probably it's because Gabriel chose me from day one, and now I've chosen him for every day forward.

SEVENTEEN
GABRIEL

"They have my number, and they'll consider my request for a sit-down," I announce after ending the call.

"That was fast." Caleb starts pacing, biting at his thumbnail.

"That's how the Operator works."

His brow is furrowed as if he doubts that. I can't blame him. We have a right, and probably an obligation, to be suspicious of everyone at this moment. "Did you talk to Navarro himself?"

"No, to his right hand. Mateo Estrada." A young-sounding Mexican guy with a smooth voice and a surprisingly pleasant demeanor. Not that that means he's above brutally murdering his enemies along with their loved ones.

"Oh, you mean the prick that was probably in our club last night, holding a bag over Mike's head?" Caleb collects a mouthful of smoke and releases it in a perfect ring. "The sooner I can kill the fucker, the better."

"We're trying to work a truce, Caleb," I remind him.

"So what? We just let them get away with killing Mike? No, there needs to be retribution."

He sounds like our father. And, truth be told, the need for revenge is burning inside me, too. But if we hit back, when will it end? "I don't know. What I *do* know is that we can't have a repeat of Vegas."

He throws his hands in the air. "Solved some big problems, delivered some long-needed justice, didn't it?"

"And created some new, potentially bigger ones." A triple murder in our hotel room, with witnesses. "Do I need to do this alone?"

"Do what alone?" Mercy saunters in from her goodbyes with Michelle, hugging herself as if warding off the cold.

Instinctively I reach out for her, and she comes to me, curling her arms around my torso, nestling her face against into my neck to press a kiss there. I was ready to punch Caleb earlier for beating down my door and dragging me away from this perfect creature. All I want to do is crawl back into bed and get tangled up in her warm, naked body.

"Nothing important. Just business," Caleb says through a puff. It's his usual dismissive answer, an attempt to keep everyone in the dark. It's the same thing Dad always said to our mother. It's been ingrained in us.

But those days are over. "I have no secrets from Mercy anymore." To her, I explain what's going on, all the while ignoring Caleb's eyes burning into the side of my face.

Her forehead wrinkles with concern. "So, you're going to meet with this cartel leader who has made it clear he wants to take over your territory and who keeps killing off your people to get it, so you can ask him nicely to leave you alone?"

"Exactly!" Caleb waves his hands dramatically. "Thank you, Mercy! Please tell him what a colossally bad idea this is."

"I don't usually agree with your brother, but this doesn't sound smart, Gabriel."

I spear Caleb with a glare. "We don't have a choice. We need to look Navarro in the eye and tell him that they are welcome to take over Vlad Easton's territory. We need to hand it to him on a silver platter, and we need to do that before my father has a chance to hit back in a way that will ensure there could never be peace." Thankfully, with Bane, Ivan, and JJ gone, Dad's pool of skilled hitmen and goons has grown shallow, but if I've learned anything, it's to never underestimate him.

She pauses, biting her bottom lip in thought. "Will it be safe? For you, I mean?"

"We'll choose neutral ground, lots of witnesses." I force confidence in my voice for Mercy's benefit. Navarro is known to be a loose cannon who drinks too much and makes rash judgments, so I'm confident a meeting with him will end either with a handshake and a cigar or two deep holes for us.

"Okay." She sets her chin. "Then I'm coming, too."

Caleb bursts out with a bark of laughter. "Oh my God, you two *are* perfect for each other. You're both *insane*."

"No, Mercy—" I begin, but she cuts me off.

"If it's safe like you say it is, then there shouldn't be any issue with me being there—"

"No."

"But I—"

"*No*. You're staying here where you'll be safe."

Anger and fear flash in her eyes. "So then you just lied to me and where you're going is *not* safe, is that what you're telling me?"

I groan. She set me up for that one. "No, that's not what I'm—"

"What happened to our deal? The one where you *promised* me you wouldn't do something stupid."

"It's not stupid. It's the right move!" Frankly, it's our only option.

"And *this* is why girlfriends and wives don't get involved in our business," Caleb chirps between puffs, which earns a glare from Mercy and a surrendering gesture and shrug from him.

I'm about to holler at him to shut the hell up, when a phone chimes.

All three of us turn toward the burner resting on the bar.

Bane's phone.

My stomach tenses. Surely, there's only one person who'd be calling it. The question is, why?

"Do you think he knows? Has he figured it out?" Mercy asks with a shaky voice. I know what she's worried about—repercussions for her father.

"There's only one way to find out." Caleb takes a step toward it with grim determination on his face.

"No, wait." I throw my hand in the air. "As far as

Lewis knows, Mercy is dead and I'm buying myself time. That's all Dad will have heard, if he's been in contact with Carruthers." Our little FBI mole shares good information but he's difficult to get hold of. "But if you answer that phone, then Dad *definitely* knows that he's lost his leverage. We're not ready for that yet." Duncan Wheeler doesn't have enough protection. George has funnelled all our money into new accounts but we're still moving cash from stash houses, choking the final breaths from our father's access to protection funds.

Caleb freezes.

We all stand idle and listen to the phone ring twenty times before it stops. The silence that follows is eerie.

"How long before your—"

My phone rings, cutting off Caleb's question.

A chill runs down my spine.

The three of us share a look. It's too much of a coincidence to be anyone other than Vlad calling.

I hold my finger to my lips, put it on speaker, and answer with a "Yeah?"

"Why am I hearing about JJ and Ivan from anyone but my sons!" my father growls in greeting. He's in a pissy mood, as expected. But at least if he's focused on them, he's not thinking about Mercy.

"Because we've been too busy dealing with a triple murder inside our club office to worry about giving *you* an update," I snap. "Our manager is dead. The place is crawling with cops. They've shut us down, for who knows how long!"

"Who gives a shit about your precious club? Two of

my most trusted people have been slaughtered and all you worry about is a building that can be replaced. I should have had Bane blow that up instead of the plane. Then maybe your focus wouldn't be so divided."

"What the hell did you *think* was going to happen after Hermosillo? That Navarro'd just roll over and show you his belly like an obedient dog? Only a fool would think that."

"Watch yourself. That's bold talk for someone who's been crying over his piece of ass. Maybe Bane should give her a taste of what's to come if you don't start cooperating."

My gaze flips to Mercy, to catch the flash of recognition in her eyes, and the mix of fear and rage that bubbles. But she presses a hand over her mouth as if to plug the risk of so much as a gasp from squeaking out.

Dad's threats of Bane are impotent, but he doesn't know that yet. When he does figure it out, those threats will shift to Mercy's father. I have to keep up appearances, so I adjust my tone to something more somber. "We *have* been cooperating, haven't we? We've handled Puff, we're hunting down the Perris—"

"Navarro's daughter, Ava. I want you to take care of her."

"Are you out of your fucking mind?" Caleb, silent up until now, bursts. "We're not taking out a cartel leader's daughter. We're not taking out *anyone*'s daughter. Have Bane do it."

I spear my brother with a warning glare. That taunt doesn't help our cause.

"You afraid?" Vlad mocks.

"No, we're not stupid."

"Do you think Navarro will hesitate to kill you both because you are my sons?"

"And yet he hasn't tried. The only one who has tried to kill us is *you*," Caleb retorts.

"He hasn't tried *yet*. My sources say you're both dead men, if Navarro has his way. And the plane was a valuable lesson, so you don't get caught unaware like JJ and Ivan."

"We don't need any of your goddamn lessons—"

"Enough!" I pinch the bridge of my nose to quell the headache that their bickering spurns. Is Dad lying about his sources' intel to scare us or is Navarro planning on taking us out?

Caleb shakes his head, though Dad can't see it. "I don't care. We're not doing it."

"Then you can take responsibility for Bane carving up Gabriel's pretty little toy's face. I'll make sure he sends pictures."

Caleb sneers and opens his mouth, and I know what he's about to say—that Gabe's pretty little toy killed his pit bull and no one's ever going to touch her again. It's what I would love to say, too, but that won't help anything but our egos.

I snap a finger at him, a warning to shut up.

Caleb's mouth twists with a sour expression, but thankfully he doesn't say any more.

Flat out refusing our father is not an option, we've learned that long ago, and it's not part of the plan now. "Navarro'll have extra security on her. We won't be able to get close."

"You'll figure something out." I hear satisfaction in his voice, the sound of triumph. He assumes he has me under his thumb. "But we have a more pressing concern now. Ivan was managing the shipment. Now that he's gone, you two will need to ensure it arrives at the warehouse."

"What do you mean? You want *us* running drugs?" Caleb's face morphs with a mixture of amusement and shock. Dad and Peter *never* stepped foot at a drop location; it's way too risky. That's what Ivan and JJ were for. "No fucking way. Get one of the other guys to do it." He starts naming some of Dad's lackeys, paid to carry guns and shoot when needed.

"They can't be in charge! None of them could find their assholes in the dark. You two need to be there to make sure it all goes smoothly."

"Maybe you shouldn't have killed off Uncle Peter and his entire family then, huh?" Caleb mutters.

"Get the men in line under you and get rid of them if they're not!" Dad snaps back. "Call Puff. He'll send bodies. That's why we took his family. It's called leverage. Learn how to use it!"

Yeah, Dad's a master at wielding leverage, even on his own sons.

I sigh. No matter what objection I give, he'll have an answer for it. "It's too hot right now. The feds are all over us, and Ivan was just grilled by Navarro's men. If they got the details out of him, they could be setting a trap for us. We'll end up either dead or in that hellhole with you. We need to move the drop—"

"We're not moving the drop. It's already on its way

and Eduardo does not take well to chaos," Dad cuts in. "Our two biggest dealers are waiting and if we don't get them product, they'll go to Navarro. They've told me as much. So no, this delivery is happening and you two are going to personally manage it."

One of the steps creaks. I look up to see Mercy disappear up the stairs, her long, slender legs carrying her swiftly, as if she can't get away fast enough. I hadn't realized she'd peeled away. Is it about the meeting with Navarro? Is it about this phone call? About the casual threats my father tossed around?

Maybe all of it.

"Gabriel!" Dad barks, grabbing my attention.

"I gotta go, something came up."

"What do you mean 'something came up'?" Dad sputters. "We have things to discuss—"

I end the call and toss my phone on the counter.

"Oh, man, he's going to be *pissed*." Caleb chuckles.

"He's already pissed." Maybe I shouldn't have been so abrupt and cavalier, especially when Dad needs to keep believing he has my balls in his fist, but I'm tired of this game.

Sure enough, my phone rings. I can practically feel him seething. I let it ring until it cuts off.

Seconds later, Bane's phone rings again.

I meet my brother's gaze, my rage churning.

"Dad doesn't bluff about certain things."

Like when he threatens to carve up a person's face.

"He's also not stupid." Caleb gives me a knowing look.

Dad's going to keep calling that phone, until he

finally clues in that something's wrong: there must be good reason Bane isn't answering. And then he's going to start getting suspicious, wondering why his son would have the nerve to blow him off like that.

And then he's going to shift his focus to Duncan Wheeler and pull whatever strings he has left to get his grubby hands on him.

My gaze trails up the stairs. I can't make Vlad Easton happy, and I don't care to try anymore. Mercy, on the other hand, I want to make happy for the rest of our lives. That's becoming clearer to me every day. But if we don't deal with Vlad Easton now, he'll hurt Mercy in ways that won't ever heal, that she won't ever forgive me for. I can't sit around and wait for that to happen. We might not have all the pieces in place but we have enough to make a move.

"There's a reason Dad never let Mom near the business and Mom never asked questions." Caleb lights up another cigarette, his tone suddenly somber. "Mercy knows too much. You're putting her in danger."

"She was kidnapped by Bane. She was *already* in danger. And she knows a lot, but she hasn't done anything. She's innocent."

"And the feds have already tried to use her father against her once."

"She's proven herself. She chose me."

"And if DeHavilland can't get his conviction overturned? You think she'll choose you a second time when the feds come around again?"

"What the fuck are you trying to tell me, Caleb?" I snap. "You don't want me to be happy?"

He holds his hands in the air in a sign of surrender. "Hey, calm down. I'm just trying to look out for you guys. You and I both know Lewis won't be the last agent to come at her. The hard-on they've had for us will not shrink once Dad's gone."

He's right about that. "So, what am I supposed to do then?"

"Don't tell her more than she needs to know. At least about what's about to go down."

"And as far as what she already knows?"

He smirks. "I hear city hall throws a mean wedding."

Jesus. I snort. "Are you kidding me?"

The smirk falls off. "No, actually, I'm not. How long before Lewis picks her up again? We have all these chess pieces lined up in order to get out from under Dad's thumb, and in the end, Mercy might be the one who sinks us. And she won't even mean to."

"I don't have time for that conversation right now." I've thought about it more than once. I was in the middle of asking her to give up her apartment and move in with me permanently when Caleb barged into the bathroom. "And, besides, Mercy would laugh in my face at the suggestion of marriage." Even joking about her becoming Mrs. Pink Panther back in Vegas earned me a tirade of all the reasons I'm not marriage material. And that was *before* feeling the wrath of Lewis and Bane.

"Yeah, fine. But you better start thinking about it soon. In the meantime, what do you want to do about that delivery? If someone's not there to greet the truck, we'll have made an enemy of Eduardo and I don't know about you but one cartel boss hunting us down is enough for me."

"Yeah, but if what Dad said is true about Navarro looking to take us out, then there's a chance his men will be waiting for us. How do we know Ivan or JJ didn't give it up? I don't know if I trust either to keep their mouths shut when they're being tortured, do you?" It's too risky.

"So then come on with the bright ideas, little brother, because I'm fresh out." He shakes his head. "We set these wheels in motion when you dragged me down to the cellar that night. We can't slow this fucking train down now. Someone's got to be there to meet the truck."

"You're right." I collect my phone. "Then let's make sure someone's there to meet it. And we need to pull the trigger on the rest of the plan. This ends now."

EIGHTEEN
MERCY

I SHUT my eyes and focus on the sound of the various showerheads spraying my sore body.

Hoping it'll drown out the echo of that monster's hateful voice as he rattled off demands of retribution and murder like he's ordering breakfast off a menu. And not just murder of the criminal element. Someone's daughter.

I couldn't listen to him anymore. That man had me kidnapped. That man granted Bane a license to torment me as he saw fit.

That man is the reason I now have blood on my hands.

I need this nightmare to be over, but will it ever be? Truly? It's not just Vlad Easton that's the issue. They've got suppliers and dealers and people within the organization that must have a lot to lose if Gabriel and Caleb walk away. Will they earn themselves more enemies, to add to the scary ones who already want them dead?

But one problem at a time, I guess and that problem

is still very much Vlad Easton, insulated in his little concrete cocoon, dialing numbers and issuing threats that I know aren't idle. He's going to figure out that Bane is dead soon enough.

My father is a sitting duck in there.

A painful lump forms in my throat with that thought.

The bathroom door slides shut with a soft thud and I jump.

"It's just me," Gabriel calls out at the same time I turn to find him standing there, his eyes rolling over my naked body. But again, I don't see the usual lust burning in them that I've become accustomed to. It's probably because he can see where Bane touched me. My thighs and arms and back are marred with dark spots where that lunatic's fingers dug into my flesh while tossing me around.

"Didn't you just have a bath?"

I tip my head back under the showerhead. "I needed to wash the sunscreen off me."

Behind me, the rustling of jeans and thump of shoes being kicked off tells me Gabriel is joining me in here, just like he used to before the door to his world was pushed wide open and I got a good look at the evil beyond.

In moments, strong hands are sliding up and down my biceps. It's a soothing, gentle touch as if he's afraid any more will hurt me "Are you okay?" Concern laces his voice.

"I was just thinking about how much easier it was, back when I was in the dark and I hated your guts."

A few beats of silence meet my words. He leans in against me, his tall, muscular body pressing into mine, from my shoulders all the way down to our feet. "Are you saying that you have regrets?" There's an odd sorrow in his tone that pricks my chest.

"No. I don't believe in regrets."

"What do you believe in then?"

"Learning from my mistakes."

He steers my body around until I'm facing him, his index finger slipping under my chin to guide my eyes to his. In them, I see a vulnerability that he normally hides so well behind a stormy blue gaze and a hard jaw. He can't hide it from me anymore. I've gotten to know him too well. "Am I a mistake?"

"Without you, my father would be dead."

"And if he ends up dead anyway, because of this? Then will I have been a mistake?" he asks quietly.

Tears stream down my cheeks and while the water washes them away, he must know I'm crying. I don't know the answer to that. Yes, a million times yes, falling in love with Gabriel Easton was the biggest mistake I could ever have made in my life, because now I can't just walk away—not after Agent Lewis's threats, not after my kidnapping, not with whatever future or lack of future there is ahead of us. "If you are, you're one I could never have avoided, and I don't think I'll ever learn from it."

He collects my cheek in his palm, his other arm curling around my waist, pulling our bodies flush again, front to front. It's only been days since we've been intimate and yet it feels like forever since that night in

Vegas, overlooking the terrace. "My father is not getting what he wants from us. He'll be dealt with soon."

"Before he hurts my father? Or worse?"

"Your father's in solitary until this is over. I just spoke to Donny and he confirmed it."

"Solitary didn't protect Fleet's cousin," I remind him with knowing glare.

"That was different. *No one* is getting to him, I promise. You have to trust me on this, Mercy."

"I *do* trust you. I just…." I release a shaky breath. A cell on his own? What must be going through my father's head right now?

"We've cut our father off his money. He has nothing substantial left to bribe anyone with, and that message is filtering through the entire prison. It'll take some time for it to resonate but when it does, there's a long line of enemies waiting for him. And then we'll set a truce with Navarro and deal with anyone else who might want to give us trouble. I'm going to get us far away from this world." He caps that pledge off with a tender kiss.

Is that fool's hope though? "I *can't* live like this for the rest of my life, Gabriel," I whisper. "Worrying about agents trying to turn me against you, or some lunatic ambushing me in my home—"

"No one's going to lay a hand on you ever again. I'd kill them if they tried. But no one will have any reason to. Except me." His hand slips down between us, his knuckle teasing my nipple. It reacts accordingly, pebbling beneath his touch. "DeHavilland will get your father's case dropped and this nightmare you've been living for too long will be over."

I want to believe him. "And then what?"

His bottom lip pulled between his teeth in thought. "You know a lot of things, Mercy. Things that could get you into trouble with Lewis or the next agent who decides to make their career off the Easton name."

"I'm not going to tell them anything—"

"I know." He abandons his teasing touch to scoop my face in his palms. "But I don't want to give them the opportunity to use what you know against you." He hesitates. "So I think we should get married."

My jaw drops.

"Just hear me out before you say no." He pauses, his gaze rolling over my features, as if soaking them in. "If we're married, no one can use you against me, and they'd have a hard time fabricating a case against you."

It's not the first time Gabriel's mentioned marriage but the last time he did it, it was in the context of teasing. Not serious.

Now, he sounds genuine.

"That's not why people get married," I hear myself say, a rush of adrenaline flooding through me.

"Normal people, no, but we don't lead normal lives, Mercy."

"I know, but—"

"What do you need to hear? That you're unlike any other woman I've ever met, that I would give up my freedom and my life for you, that all it took was thinking I'd lost you for a few days to know I will follow you anywhere in this life and into the next, hopefully many years from now." He leans in to plant a soft kiss against my collarbone.

I shudder as his fine stubble scrapes over my skin.

"I know I'm not good enough for you, but I'm trying to be. And together, we can live the kind of life you deserve. We can do whatever we want. Go wherever we want." One of his hands curls around my back. The other shifts down over my belly, between my legs, his fingertip goading my body to respond. A rush of blood flows downward toward my core. "The mountains, an island, on a yacht in the middle of the ocean. Europe, the Caribbean…." He slips two fingers deep inside me and a moan escapes my lips. "Have you ever been to Malta?"

I push aside all my worries for the moment and let myself become immersed by Gabriel's skillful touch and enchanting words. Days ago, hanging from a chain in a shed, I didn't think I'd ever see him again, let alone be talking about a future. "I've never been anywhere."

"We have more than enough money to start a whole new life, anywhere we want."

"That's your money, not mine." And it's dirty money. Would I ever have the stomach to reconcile that fact?

He peels his mouth away from my neck to meet my eyes. "Haven't you figured it out yet? Everything I have is yours." The muscle in his jaw ticks. "Including my heart. That's yours. It'll never be anyone else's."

Who is this man? He's Gabriel with his wandering, assertive hands and bullish style, but he's gentler, softer, vulnerable.

My hand automatically shifts to his chest, the steady beat thumping against my palm. So strong and vibrant.

"And what if I don't want to go anywhere? What if I want to stay in Phoenix and keep working at Mary's Way?" He's never seen the value in me spending my days surrounded by people who fall prey to the very thing his family peddles. The more I think about it now though, especially seeing this side of him, I wonder if his disdain is borne from guilt more than anything to do with those people's weakness.

The corner of his mouth twitches. "This feels like a test."

"Maybe it is."

He studies me carefully. "And let me guess, we'd be making a lot of donations to keep Mary's Way open?"

"Yearly. Huge ones."

He curses under his breath, but by the gleam in his eye, I know he's just playing the part. "Like I said, I'll follow you anywhere, Mercy. Even to Mary's Way." He caps that off with a deep kiss against my lips. "Say yes and DeHavilland will get us the paperwork and an appointment with a judge first thing in the morning."

A flutter of nerves explodes in my stomach. "In the morning? As in *tomorrow morning*? You want to get married *tomorrow morning*."

"Lewis is going to show up again soon and when she sees all your bruises, she's going to pull out every trick in that oversized purse of hers. I don't want her being able to put you through that again."

My gut clenches at the thought of being cornered in a room by that woman again.

"And there's a lot of shit that's about to go down in

the next few days. I want to make sure you're protected in every way."

A bubble of laughter erupts in my throat. "You're insane."

He smirks. "You knew this."

"I did." Given our history, this latest proposal of his is not all that shocking. If anything, it's endearing.

"Please say yes," He begs.

Exhilaration builds in my chest. The word is on the tip of my tongue, the impulse overwhelming. "Just let me think about it, please? For more than five minutes."

"Fine. But while you're thinking…." He backs me against the shower wall and lifts me by the back of my legs, lining our bodies up.

This is what Gabriel does: fucks me into submission, getting his way every time. As much as I want him inside me, I reach down and grasp his hard length with my fist, stalling him. "*If* I say yes to this, nothing changes between us."

He swallows hard. "I feel like *a lot* would change between us."

I squeeze. "I mean, you don't control me; you don't own me."

He groans. "Are you kidding? *You* own *me*. You have since the moment I laid eyes on you."

My pulse quickens, but I don't let myself get derailed. "And you are out of your father's world for good. You have to be."

"After we get through these next few days and I do what I *need* to do." He levels me with a look that says I won't like any of it.

"Right. After that."

"*Please* say yes, Mercy," he whispers, capturing my lips in mine, adjusting his hold of my thighs to widen my hips.

I guide him into me without giving him an answer.

I know what it'll be.

THE HUM of the Lamborghini's engine competes with the whir of my nerves in my stomach as we drive along Camelback Road. It's 7:00 a.m., but the sky is a pretty cornflower blue and the heat is already building.

Gabriel's eyes leave the road ahead to meet mine. Our hands are clasped together in a tight weave, resting on the stick. He drags his thumb across my wrist, where the bruises from Bane are suitably hidden beneath layers of carefully applied foundation. It took me nearly an hour to cover all the marks that madman left. "You look beautiful."

I smooth a hand over the pale blush-colored material of my dress. It was Michelle's Kentucky Derby dress as she likes to call it; a fitted asymmetrical outfit that reaches to my knees and ties at the waist—and the only thing in my closet that seemed appropriate for a trip to Scottsdale's city hall to marry a crime boss's son so I can avoid being summoned in any potential cases the feds are building against him.

I can't believe I'm doing this but given what I know about Gabriel and his family, it's either the smartest or dumbest decision I've made in a long time.

"It's not too much?"

"Too much clothing? Yeah, but I'll fix that as soon as we get home." He brings my hand to his mouth, to press a kiss against the back of it. There's an odd, serene smile touching his lips when he settles our hands on the stick again.

"What's that smile for?"

It grows wider, his eyes crinkling at the corners. "I don't know. I guess I'm just happy."

"So am I," I admit, adjusting the collar of his crisp white button-down. Never in a million years could I have predicted that the menacing criminal I locked eyes with in Fulcort's visitor room would be someone I'd fall madly in love with. "I just wish my father could be here for it." Not that he'd ever in a million years approve, but in the grand scheme of things, this seems like the least crazy thing I've done these past weeks. One day, I'll fill him in… maybe.

"So then, we don't tell anyone, and when this is all said and done, and your father is out, we can have something more formal."

"That's not a bad idea." I snort. "And I'm sure Caleb would be happy about that." He was standing in the kitchen in his briefs and a gaping silk robe when we left the house, still high, shoveling spoonfuls of cereal in his mouth. When he realized where we were going, his jaw practically hit the floor. He insisted on being a witness, but we didn't have time to wait for him. Besides, DeHavilland and his partner are meeting us at the courthouse to fill that role, after plying a judge and clerk with wads of cash to issue the license and perform the ceremony outside of regular hours.

"Caleb won't be invited."

I laugh. "Shut up. He'll be your best man."

"Trust me, you don't want that." Gabriel smirks. "Every wedding he's ever been a guest at, he ends up naked and fucking someone. One time, it was the bride's mother…." His words drift, his steely eyes flickering back and forth between the road and his rear-view mirror.

"What's wrong?"

His brow furrows. "I think we're being followed."

My pulse jumps as I check the sideview mirror. "Which one?"

"Navy SUV with the tinted windows." Gabriel changes lanes and speeds up.

I watch as the vehicle mimics the move.

With a sharp curse, he grabs his phone and dials a number before putting it to his ear. "We got a tail." He recites the plate number and then ends the call.

"Farley?"

"Yeah. They're on their way." He shakes his head, anger marring his handsome face. "I should have listened to him. We should have taken the Lincoln and a team of guys. I just figured it was early and only a twelve-minute drive. I wasn't thinking straight." His jaw tenses, his eyes flipping to the mirror again. "At least they're hanging back."

"FBI?"

"Doesn't look like a government plate, but I fucking hope so."

Because if it's not her, then it's probably someone we don't want to meet. My heart hammers against my chest as Gabriel weaves around the morning traffic and I watch our shadow from the mirror.

Gabriel's phone rings a few minutes later. He answers it in an instant with a "yeah," only to hang up a moment later, his face stony. "Your seatbelt is on?"

"Of course."

The engine roars as he gives the car gas, and the odometer climbs.

My hands are balled into fists as we race down the road at double the speed limit, earning angry horn blasts as Gabriel cuts people off. At the last minute he makes a hard right turn. The wheels screech as we veer and then we're flying down a quiet residential street of white stucco bungalows and looming palm trees. Few people are out this early, which is a small blessing.

"Did we lose them?" I ask in a panic, taking turns between checking the sideview mirror and looking over my shoulder. "I think we lost—"

The SUV whips around the corner behind us, squashing the speck of relief.

Gabriel speeds toward the intersection. Early morning walkers and their dogs scuttle away from the curb with alarmed faces.

"Who are they?"

"Either Puff's people, which I highly doubt because they wouldn't have the balls to chase me, or guys my father still has in his pocket, or Navarro's guys."

A gang, a disgruntled crime boss, or a cartel. *Great.*

We're approaching an intersection with a busier cross street where the stream of cars is sparse but steady. Gabriel isn't slowing. I bite back my scream as we careen and merge, swerving to avoid a collision with a pickup truck.

Gabriel isn't just a rich prick who bought a car he can't handle. He's maneuvering around traffic like a seasoned race car driver. Still, a cold sweat coats my skin, the knowledge that all it takes is a car to change lanes to cause a wreck.

"Hold on!"

I let out a squeal and brace myself as we cut across two lanes of oncoming traffic to make a sharp left turn. We're moving in the opposite direction of Scottsdale's city hall, away from the busy streets to a quiet commercial area of small offices that haven't yet started their day. The mountain looms on our left.

Gabriel's phone rings. He answers and shouts, "Where the fuck are you?"

"Four minutes out if you slow down!" Comes Farley's muffled response through the speaker.

He ends the call, his eyes on the rearview mirror. After a lingering look, he takes his foot off the gas and engine quiets back to a rumbling purr.

"What do they want?'

"Doesn't matter. They're not getting it," he says, his voice taking on that hard, cool tone that used to intimidate me. "I think we lost them. I don't see them anywhere back—Shit!" Gabriel slams on the brakes and the Lamborghini comes to a screeching halt.

My seatbelt snaps tight across my chest.

Mere feet away from the hood, a white Suburban that pulled out from a cross street blocks the lanes.

Gabriel doesn't waste time, throwing the car into reverse and stomping on the gas.

Only to slam on the brakes again as two more SUVs race up from behind, boxing us in. "It's an ambush," he says far too calmly, reaching beneath his seat to pull out a handgun.

From the Suburban, four men in black clothes spill out, all carrying guns.

A line of weapons aim at our windshield. "Get out of the car!" One of them yells.

Gabriel surveys the situation with calculating eyes. "Farley will be here any minute."

Movement in the sideview window catches my eyes. More men with guns are trickling out of the other vehicles, surrounding us. "Gabriel—"

"I know. I see them. Just stay where you are."

"Get out of the car!" The man bellows again. He dips the tip of his gun downward and fires a round into the hood of the Lamborghini. It's a warning shot.

Gabriel hisses with anger.

A man sidles up to my window and taps the glass with the barrel of his gun. It's inches away from my temple. My heart, already racing, pounds in my throat.

"Last chance! Get out of the car or she's dead!"

Gabriel's jaw tenses. "Listen to me, carefully. They want me, not you."

"What does that mean?"

"Do what they say, and don't say a word. Don't fight back. Do you understand?"

I swallow against my terror. He didn't answer my question. "Yes."

Slowly, he sets his gun on the dash and, showing his hands, he hits the door locks.

The next few moments happen in a terrifying blur of shouts and forceful hands, until Gabriel and I are on our knees in front of his car, the barrels of seven guns trained on us and nowhere to run.

From the backseat of the Suburban, a curvy woman in a stylish poppy-colored suit steps out. Jet black heels that match her sleek hair color click on the pavement as she approaches us, a confident stride in her steps. She's young—in her late-twenties, I'm guessing—and beautiful, and not hinting at an ounce of trepidation. "Gabriel Easton," she purrs, her accent elongating the vowels from his name with melodic flare. "I hear you have been trying to reach my father."

"Your father." Gabriel exhales slowly. "You *must* be Ava Navarro."

I've heard that name before, just last night. This is the daughter Vlad wants them to kill. I assumed she was a child. An innocent.

"Why do you want to meet with him?"

"That's between him and me," Gabriel answers smoothly.

Her lips twist as if she's tasted something sour. In her coal black eyes, a challenge gleams. "Wrong answer. You have three seconds to provide the right one." She nods to one of the men and he closes the distance toward me, unsheathing a curved blade from his hip.

My bladder threatens to unleash.

"One—" She begins, her voice hard and uncompromising.

Gabriel's jaw tenses. "My brother and I want a truce."

She pauses. "And does Vlad Easton want a truce?"

"No. He wants us to kill you."

"What a coincidence. My father has plans to kill you."

"If you do that, I can promise, there isn't a place in this world you'll be able to hide from Caleb."

"I guess we shall see." She snaps her fingers.

A dull thud sounds beside me. My jaw drops in horror as Gabriel falls forward to the ground, a scream bubbling in my throat but unable to escape. The man behind him holds his gun in reverse. They didn't shoot him, I tell myself. They only knocked him unconscious. He's still alive. For now.

"Get up." Someone jabs me in the back as two men hoist Gabriel off the ground and drag him toward the SUV, his limp legs dragging on the road behind him.

Without any other choice—not that I'd leave Gabriel's side—I let them lead me into the back seat.

NINETEEN
GABRIEL

The steady whir of a ceiling fan is the first sound I process as my eyelids crack open. My head throbs. Whoever drilled my skull is going to regret that—

Mercy.

I bolt up to a sitting position, only to lurch forward, nausea roiling in my stomach. I take a few deep breaths to stop from puking and moments to process the four-poster bed and the posh bedroom. Wherever I am, at least it's not a dirty cell.

A low murmur snaps my head to my left, to the door where a man stands, a phone pressed to his ear, a gun in his free hand. He's the dickhead standing behind me when we got out of the car, and likely the one who thumped me.

"Where's my girlfriend?" I croak, my voice still unsteady after being knocked unconscious. My girlfriend who should be my wife. We would have been married by now, if not for these fucking clowns.

He ends the call with a "Sí," and opens the door. "Follow me."

I pull myself to my feet, pausing to smooth my palm over my rumpled shirt, when really I need a moment to steel my wobbly legs before I stumble like a newborn foal.

"Come," he beckons, guiding me with a wave of his gun.

"Yeah, yeah." I follow his directions, stepping out into a long window-lined hallway. Through the glass, rolling hills and green landscape stretch in every direction. This isn't Arizona. "Where is the woman I was with?" I ask again.

My guard trails behind me. "Do not cause problems and you will see her again. Cause problems and you will see her again, but it will not be under pleasant circumstances."

If you touch her, your death will be slow and painful. I stifle the urge to threaten him—he's just a lackey—and instead focus on my surroundings. The house I'm in is a modern, spacious place of sand-colored travertine stone and beige walls. I'm guessing southern California, somewhere near the Mexican border.

He leads me down one side of an elaborate dual staircase with wrought-iron railings and around a corner. An armed man opens a set of double doors and shifts aside, his hands at the ready on his gun.

Inside, I find an impressive office lined with mahogany bookshelves and decorated with large, broad-leafed plants. And Ava Navarro, perched on the edge of a desk, arms folded across her ample chest, all prim and proper as if posing for a business magazine cover.

"Gabriel Easton," she announces again, my name sounded more like "Gabrielle" on her tongue.

"If you've hurt her, everyone you've ever loved will die." The warning slips out without a thought and in that moment, I mean it.

Maybe I'm not so different from my father after all.

She studies me for a long moment before commanding, "Leave us."

"But, Ava," the man who escorted me here begins to say.

"It's alright, Tony. He isn't foolish enough to lay a hand on me," she says to him, though her gaze never leaves mine.

The door clicks shut behind me.

"Your reputation precedes you." Her dark eyes drag over my body, stalling just below my belt before drifting back up, a knowing smirk touching her lips. "I've heard much about Vlad Easton's sons, pretty men who love women and fast cars and little responsibility. He's kept you distant from his empire, aside from laundering money with your nightclub."

"You've done two seconds of research. Good for you," I drawl.

She slides off the desk and makes a point of walking slowly around it, her shapely hips swaying with each step. "Tell me, I wonder what you have heard about me?"

It's my turn to smirk. "Not much, to be honest. I didn't even know you were working for your father." I'd heard Luiz had two children. His eldest—a son—was murdered by Eduardo in one of their cartel turf wars years ago, leaving him with a teenaged daughter.

She's no teenager anymore.

I will admit, Ava Navarro is a stunning woman, with sharp cheekbones and an angular jaw and curves that can make a dick hard with just a thought, and if Mercy weren't in my life, she's exactly the type of woman I'd be aiming to bend over a table within the hour.

But all I want to do is wrap my hands around her neck and squeeze the life out of her slowly until she gives me back my heart.

"Yes, that is precisely how my father would like to keep it." Her tone is bitter. "I have spent years within the organization, learning the rules and earning the men's respect. But I am a woman and his daughter, and he is only amusing my lofty ambitions, I know this. Now that he is aging and looking toward the future of this business, he is entrusting his righthand man with everything."

"Mateo Estrada."

"Yes, the man you spoke to on the phone yesterday about a sit down with my father to discuss a truce."

"So, you knew why I wanted to see him."

"Of course I knew, though I don't yet know why. Just like I know that neither my father nor Mateo are interested in any sort of truce with the Easton organization." She rounds the desk. "Camillo Perri and the more formidable of his sons have been conveniently dispatched. Quite clever on your part, by the way, to make it look like us. Peter Easton and his sons have vanished, and the rumor is that they will not be found. And my connections in the prison tell me people are lining up to slide a knife across Vlad Easton's wrinkly old jugular. So why would my father negotiate to take over two notable empires when your family has made it so easy for them to claim the entire southwest territory in a sweeping show of force?"

"Less blood and turmoil this way? No conflict?"

"It seems you have *not* done *your* two seconds of research. If you had, you would know that my father loves blood and turmoil, and he feeds off conflict." She stalls at the window, gazing out it. "The love for that is what killed my brother and weakened my mother's heart until she, too, died." There's a forlorn quality to her voice, a lingering sadness.

And I think I'm beginning to see where this conversation is going. "Does your father know you've brought me here?"

Her steps are measured as she strolls toward me. "If my father knew I brought you here, you and your lovely woman would already be dead." She stops in front of me and my nostrils fill with a pleasing mix of jasmine and suede as she reaches up. Her finger pokes the back of my skull.

I wince at the sting from her touch, jerking my head away.

When she pulls back, her index finger is coated with bright blood. She tsks, but doesn't seem otherwise bothered by the sight. "Tell me, what terms were you going to offer my father for this truce?"

This is a gamble, but my gut tells me I'm reading the

situation right. "We were going to tell him to take all of it."

Her eyes flash. "All?"

"Our territory, the Perri territory, all of it. We don't want any of it."

Her lips hang parted for a moment and I fight the urge to laugh. She wasn't expecting that. "You don't want the family business *at all*?"

"No. We want to go strictly legitimate. Real estate, clubs, possibly a casino."

Another flash of interest in her eyes betrays her. Her throat bobs with a hard swallow as she processes this bombshell. "But Vlad would never allow this."

"No. And that's why my father needs to die."

A smile stretches across Ava's face, slowly at first, until it blooms into a beautiful, wide grin that displays pristinely white teeth. "What a coincidence. So does my mine."

TWENTY
MERCY

THE STOUT MAN who led me to the bedroom where I've spent the last hour now directs me down the set of spiral stairs, to the main floor of the house. His gun is tucked in his holster and his steps are leisurely but I'm no fool. If I ran, I wouldn't get far. I've seen the outside of this hillside mansion from the helicopter. There are men with guns crawling all around it. Besides, I promised Gabriel I would do exactly what they tell me and right now they're telling me to walk.

I clear my throat to steady my voice. "Where is Gabriel?" They carried him away, still unconscious and bleeding from a wound to the back of his head. "Please tell me if he's okay?" Seeing him like that—incapacitated and vulnerable—twisted my chest.

The man gestures toward an open set of doors with his palm raised.

At least they haven't manhandled me like Bane did. They've been nothing but courteous. I'm guessing that's because I haven't given them reason to use force.

I gingerly step inside.

"Gabriel!" I let out a cry of relief and rush toward where he sits on the couch, his head tilted forward as a young man hovers behind him, his fingers working with skilled precision to stitch up the gash. I drop to my knees in front of him.

"Un momento por favor." The doctor pulls through one last thread and then steps away to begin collecting bloody gauze and his tools. In moments, he's gone.

Gabriel collects my face in his hands. "Are you okay? They didn't hurt you?" His voice is husky, his eyes are wild with a mixture of panic and relief.

"I'm fine. How are you?"

His chest heaves with a sigh. "Five stitches and probably a concussion. All of which was totally unnecessary. As was the bullet to the engine of my car." His sharp eyes cut to the other side of the room.

I follow the gaze and find Ava Navarro sitting in the chair behind the desk, her head cocked, her chin resting on a raised hand. I hadn't noticed her when I stumbled in, too focused on getting to Gabriel.

She's studying us through intelligent dark eyes. There's genuine curiosity in that gaze. What is it about us that interests her so? And should I be afraid? Nothing in Gabriel's demeanor hints at an answer, either way.

I'm intimidated by her, that much I know.

After a moment, she gives a nonchalant shrug. "How was I supposed to know our goals would align so perfectly?"

"That remains to be seen." Gabriel pulls me onto

the couch beside him, curling a protective arm around my shoulders.

I sink into his side as Ava's phone rings. She answers it with a few murmured words in Spanish before hanging up. "Your brother will be here momentarily." Her eyes twinkle with anticipation. "Merrick and Vince Perri are with him."

A barely audible sigh escapes Gabriel that only I can hear. "Why do you need them here?" His tone is cold and stony. He doesn't trust her.

Another shrug. "If it is as you say and neither of them will challenge me with the territory, then I would like to hear it from them myself."

"*Or* you're planning on executing all of us at once."

My stomach clenches. Afraid, it is. After all, this woman's father wants Gabriel and Caleb dead. She said so herself.

She rests her elbows on the desk and studies her fingernails. Her bright red nail polish matches her suit. "Now why would I have my doctor stitch you up only to execute you? And in my own personal estate, no less."

"I don't know. You're a Navarro. I've heard things."

"And you are an Easton. I've heard things as well. Should we believe everything we hear?" she throws back, a touch of irritation in her voice.

They level each other with a hard stare.

What does Gabriel think of this woman who hunted us down and forced us out of our car at gunpoint?

Just as quickly, she seems to snap out of her foul mood with a broad smile. "Excuse my rudeness. You two must be hungry. My chef has been busy in the kitchen.

Let me see what he can prepare for us to eat." She reaches for a phone and dials, taking her attention off us for the moment.

"Do you know where we are?" I whisper.

Gabriel smooths a hand over my knee. "We're near Temecula, California. About an hour's drive from the border."

I steal a glance Ava's way. "Do we need to be worried?"

He regards the woman across the room. "She and her father don't see eye to eye."

"So, she *doesn't* want you dead?"

"I don't think so. And, if I'm right, she might solve a lot of problems for us."

"And if you're wrong?"

"Then we're climbing into bed with a poisonous snake." He offers me a wry smile. "But it still might work to our advantage."

The drone of a helicopter approaches as she's ending her call. "The kitchen is whipping up something special for us. I hope you brought your appetites with you."

Gabriel snorts. "Actually, I think I left mine back on the pavement in Arizona."

She rolls her eyes and curses in Spanish, then looks to me. "He's not going to let that go anytime soon, is he?"

"Probably not." Neither am I.

She laughs as if my answer is amusing. Her gaze rolls over my dress, the silky blush-colored hemline now tarnished by dirt and dust. "You look lovely."

"Thank you."

"Where were you two going, looking so lovely so early in the morning?"

"Had a meeting with my lawyer," Gabriel says without skipping a beat.

We were getting married. We should be married. Gabriel should be my husband. But he is clearly not offering more information to this woman than is necessary.

Her pristinely groomed eyebrow arches and I know she doesn't buy that vague answer. "Well, hopefully you can reschedule your *meeting* once we've sorted all this out."

A knock sounds on the door, just before it swings open and Caleb strolls through. Gone are the bleary eyes, briefs, and silk robe. He's dressed in a collared shirt and dress pants, and looks as stylish as he does heading in to Empire for work, minus the tie. Merrick and Vince saunter behind him —all picture-perfect versions of calm and cool and arrogance, as if they're not facing off with a deadly enemy.

When Caleb sees us sitting on the couch, his shoulders visibly sink.

"Hello, my name is Ava Navarro." She stands to greet them, pulling her shoulders back. "It's a pleasure to meet you."

Caleb's blue eyes rake over her body and I catch the appreciative glint—one can only imagine what types of filthy thoughts are cycling through his mind—but when he meets her gaze again, there's something unnerving and lethal in his gaze. "Gabe?"

"All good."

He surveys the rest of the room and the two men with guns who have positioned themselves along the perimeter of the room. His gun holster is empty, as are Merrick and Vince's. Not surprising. And probably for the best, given what happened the last time Caleb was armed and in a room with his enemies.

"*Please*. Sit." She gestures to a row of chairs in front of the desk.

Caleb eyes them before shifting his gaze back to her. "I think I'll stand for now. Stretch my legs. You know how it is."

"Very well." Ava's commanding voice is unwavering as she settles back in her chair. "Gabriel and I have been discussing our shared mutual interests."

"And what would those be, exactly?"

"Your desire to cut all ties to the business, and my desire to take over your territories."

All three men lose the battle to hold their steely expressions.

"Don't you mean your father's desire?" Merrick offers her an obnoxious smirk.

Her eyes narrow on the youngest Perri. "Of course, my father also has his sights set on your territories, as you well know by now. But I would prefer to operate independently from him and in a more professional manner."

"There's only one way that could happen," Vince says, a hint of curiosity in his tone.

"Yes, gentlemen, there is. And I'm dealing with that issue presently. It should be resolved *very* soon." She smiles sweetly.

It dawns on me. Ava Navarro is going to have her father killed.

Gabriel is right—she is a viper.

The men share a glance before looking to Gabriel for confirmation.

He shrugs in response. A noncommittal answer.

"Look, we all know I don't *need* to negotiate with you. Every man on this property is loyal to me because I value their lives as my father does not. The warehouse Vlad Easton had destroyed is but one of many. I have a steady pipeline of product. I *will* distribute it in your territories and, sooner or later, your buyers will purchase from me. They'll have no choice." She casts a lazy hand toward the man by the door. "I *could* order Tony to shoot you where you stand. I have no interest in doing that."

Merrick shifts his stance, and the armed men raise their guns a notch as if preparing for his sudden attack. The smirk he flashes is knowing and arrogant. "So then what *do* you have an interest in?"

Ava's eyes glide over his muscular frame as blatantly as Caleb just ogled her. "Your help negotiating a peaceful transition between your networks and mine. Your buyers will become my buyers, your dealers will move my product."

"That'll be kind of hard, after your father turned that Mamba into a festive pig," Vince says dryly.

"Those families will be compensated for that atrocity. I give you my word."

"I don't trust you," Caleb announces, having quietly listened to the exchange. "And I don't make deals with people I don't trust."

Ava leans back in her chair, toying with a pen as she regards him. "You have a shipment arriving today from Eduardo Velez."

"So, Ivan *did* talk," Gabriel murmurs from beside me, to no one in particular.

"Your man sang like a songbird with its wings on fire, from what I've heard. And now my father's men are preparing to ambush the delivery and slaughter whoever's there."

Caleb and Gabriel exchange a wordless look—they were right to push back with their father.

"And did you know that about a week ago Vic Easton contacted my father through the operator? He was attempting to forge a business deal for his family, one that did *not* include *your* family. My father was intrigued, of course, so he took the call."

A memory stirs in my mind, from that day in the shed, hanging from chains. Vic mentioned something about the sun setting and no one getting what he wanted. A punishment for not only Vlad but Gabriel and Caleb as well, from the sounds of it.

Caleb eases into the chair across from Ava's desk. "Please, tell us more."

Merrick and Vince fan out but stay on their feet, watching this unfold. Or maybe this is their covert attempt to move closer to the men with guns.

Tension slides down my spine with the fear that bullets might start flying any moment.

"Vic wanted to negotiate a deal with my father to buy supply from us instead of Eduardo. In exchange for that, he offered all kinds of information about you two, and about your father's most valuable soldiers. He was a fool, of course, assuming my father was an honorable man. He has no interest in working with *any* Easton, but he used that information for his own gain."

"Son of a bitch," Gabriel mutters under his breath.

"Vic knew how much Mike meant to our business, and that Ivan and JJ would never work for him." Caleb collects a small cube from Ava's desk and tests its weight in his palm. "Why are you telling us this?"

"That's what friends do. They help each other out. For example, I'm sure you don't want to lose three million dollars today *and* be indebted to Eduardo for the same. He's even more ruthless than my father and that is difficult."

Caleb and Gabriel cross glances a second time. An unspoken question is asked and answered.

"We have a contingency plan in place for the drop." Gabriel pauses as if to consider his next words. "If there is anyone within that crew who is loyal to you, I'd suggest you find them another assignment for the night. Discretely of course."

She dips her head. "See? Friends help each other out."

My curiosity overwhelms me. I have to bite my tongue against the urge to ask what Gabriel has planned. I don't understand what's happening here and this might be one of those times where it's best I'm kept in the dark.

Caleb sets the cube—a paperweight—down and settles into his seat, his thighs sprawled, his fingers steepled in front of him. "If you want to be my friend, you'll tell us who killed our club manager." There's a dangerous edge to his voice.

"That would be Mateo, my father's righthand man." She leans forward. "And because I want to be a *very good* friend to you, I've arranged for him to be delivered to you."

"Have you now…." Caleb's head cocks as he regards her with new interest. "Luiz will blame us for his death."

"He would, yes. And he would send people after you, if given the chance." She drags a fingernail along her collarbone, drawing his attention to her ample cleavage. "Fortunately for you, he will not be given that chance. He will be dead within the hour."

Caleb's eyebrows arch with surprise. "You're so sure you can pull this off."

"I'm sure that my father and Mateo would never suspect my intentions, and I'm sure that I have proficient men working for me."

"Abduction at gunpoint in the morning, a hit on your father by lunch. What can I say except you keep busy."

"These plans have been in motion for much longer than you might think. But no, in general, I don't waste time." Ava's dark eyes roll over Caleb's face, stalling on his mouth. "Not when I see something I want."

This woman is anything but bashful. I guess that's a requirement for a future cartel drug lord. If not for that reality, I'd say she and Caleb would be perfect for each other. But she's a stone-cold killer. She might be more dangerous than all these men, combined.

The corner of Caleb's mouth twitches. "So, then

there's only the matter of our father. He's a bit of a problem."

"Vlad Easton will be condemned for my father's murder, and I will demand his death as retribution. If you would be so kind as to lift your ring of protection around him in that prison, I'll be able to get to him more easily."

"It's already in the works."

"Then he won't last the night." She offers a seductive smile.

He studies her for a long moment. "Actually, we'd be grateful if we could see him one last time before that happens."

Playfulness flashes in her eyes. "*How* grateful?"

A genuine grin finally stretches across Caleb's lips, and those devilish dimples appear. "You want me to describe it, or can I show you?"

Oh my God. "Why do I feel like I'm watching some sort of twisted foreplay in action?" I hiss in Gabriel's ear.

He snorts. "Because you are." But I don't miss the way his body sags beside mine. He seems relieved.

This is what Gabriel and Caleb have been angling for all along—for someone to take out Vlad in Fulcort. Originally, the Perris were supposed to help with that, but that all went to hell in Vegas. And now here we are, with a solution that fits everyone's needs.

Even mine, I'll admit, because in order for my father to be safe inside, Vlad Easton has to die.

A phone rings. Ava and Caleb seem to snap out of

whatever intimate trance they were caught in, pulling themselves up straighter in their chairs.

She answers, speaking to the caller in Spanish. The call only lasts a few seconds, but when she ends it, her olive skin has paled.

"Is something wrong?" Gabriel asks.

"No. Nothing's wrong. Everything is as it should be." She reaches for a framed picture in the corner of her desk, stroking the glass with her index finger. "It's done. Luiz Navarro will no longer be an issue for either of your families. Or for mine."

I feel the blood drain from my face.

Caleb steals a glance our way, his eyebrows arched—in surprise or excitement, I can't tell.

Abruptly, Ava stands and strolls to the window, her demeanor more somber. "If you'll all excuse me, I have a few phone calls to make before we can celebrate this new friendship. Please make yourselves comfortable in my home. The pools are especially warm on this hot day."

"Actually, we have a busy schedule. I think we'll be heading off now—"

"I insist." She meets Caleb's unyielding gaze with her own. "There are still many moving parts to this arrangement. Stay for the day. For your safety, as well as mine."

"Can I at least have my phones back?" Gabriel asks evenly. "I have a few calls of my own to make."

She nods toward Tony.

"And our guns?" Merrick adds.

"Nice try." Ava's eyes rake over him again without a

hint of modesty. "We're not that good of friends… yet." She winks.

I DO my best to ignore the small army of guards—all equipped with automatic rifles—as Gabriel and I stroll along the pathway, taking in the panoramic view of the valley below and rolling hills as far as my eyes reach. Ava's estate is a palace on top of a hill, but the retaining wall that surrounds it making it feel like a fortress. Within those walls are leggy palm trees that offer little shade, interlocking pools of various shapes and sizes, one boasting a swim-up bar while another is half-covered by an artificial cave and waterfall. A variety of cozy alcoves provide ample seating—both in the sun and sheltered beneath pavilions.

The last I saw Caleb and the Perri brothers, they were beyond the gate by the helicopter pad, in deep conversation with Farley. It seems none of Gabriel and Caleb's security were permitted inside.

"How long are we expected to stay here?" I tug at the collar of my ruined dress. My sweat is soaking through the silk material. I'm ready to dive into the water, fully dressed.

"Until we're feeling extra *friendly*?" Gabriel reaches back to graze his new stitches with his finger.

I gently swat his hand away. "Does it hurt?"

"Nothing a few pills won't fix." With a wry smirk, he collects my hand in his and brings the back of it to his mouth. His lips are warm and supple against my skin.

We turn down a path that takes us toward the house and the stone-clad terrace, where staff are setting a dining table with white linens and centerpieces for an elaborate meal. Ava did say she was having the kitchen prepare food for us. It's an odd turn of events—from kidnapping at gunpoint to this—and it's left me unsettled.

"What do you know about her? Ava, I mean."

"Not much, beyond what we've heard today." He eyes the guards. "She seems smart and she's definitely ambitious. But it's the kind of ambition that gets people killed, especially when they're going up against Eduardo Velez, who's going to feel the loss of business."

The last thing I feel is sympathy for the Easton drug supplier. I just don't want it to blow back on us. "Do you trust her?"

"I only trust two people: Caleb and you."

My chest swells at that declaration. There was a time when my name didn't make that list. "But do you think she'll keep up her end of this deal you've just made?"

"We'll know soon enough. But I'm not gonna lie, getting rid of Navarro has already solved a big problem for us. *If* it actually happened. She could be full of shit. I'm waiting on my PI to confirm."

"It's real." The way her face paled, the way she reached for that picture. I caught a glimpse of it on my way out of the room. In it, she's arm in arm with an older gentleman who I'm guessing was her father.

She had her own father executed. I bite back those critical words before they slip out. Gabriel and Caleb have basically announced open season on their father. It's no different.

But Ava did it to get in deeper with her criminal world, I remind myself. Gabriel and Caleb want to get far away. There *is* a difference.

And Vlad Easton surely deserves what's coming to him.

A twisted rationale, but one I can live with.

Gabriel's phone rings. He slips it out and answers. "Yup?" His blue eyes search the premises as he listens to whoever's on the other line—a woman, by the sounds of it. "Yeah, that's my car, Special Agent Lewis."

My mouth drops. "*Why is Lewis calling you*!" I hiss.

He shushes me with an index finger against my lips.

"I heard it was stolen out of my driveway this morning, but I didn't have a chance to file a report. I'm out of town." His eyebrows arch. "A *bullet in my engine*, you say. Gosh, whoever took it must be mixed up with dangerous people."

I roll my eyes at him.

"Of course I've seen Mercy. She's right here. Do you want to say hello?" He frowns as he listens. "Why on earth would I ask someone else to pretend to be her." He smiles as he holds out his phone. His mood is light. Now that I'm safe and my father is relatively so, he's having fun with the FBI agent.

Nerves flutter in my stomach as I collect it. "Hello?"

"Mercy Wheeler?" A familiar, smooth voice asks.

"Yes," I say warily.

"My name is Special Agent Kennedy Lewis. I've been trying to reach you for days to confirm some details about last Wednesday night's plane explosion. When can we talk in person?"

She's pretending this is the first time we've ever spoken. She assumes Gabriel's listening and I haven't told him about our other meetings. Maybe she's trying to protect me, or maybe she's trying to protect her case.

Either way, I'm done with this game.

I steel my nerve. "Yes, I remember you well, Agent Lewis. You cornered me in the spa in Vegas and fed me lies about Gabriel. Then you tracked me down at the Cirque show and threatened to arrest me for crimes I never committed."

Several seconds of dead silence fills my ear.

And then, "You're making a big mistake."

Maybe.

Maybe every choice I've made since I stepped into Fulcort that day has been the wrong one. But if I had to do it all over again? The only thing I'd do differently is tell Gabriel about this woman the second she made contact.

"I'm not sure when I'll be back in town yet, but you have Gabriel's number. Let me know when you'd like to meet and I'll arrange for my lawyer to attend with me. Until then, you're cutting into my pool time."

Gabriel stifles a snort as I hand the phone back to him, my hand trembling despite my brazenness.

"I appreciate the call and your ongoing concern for my safety. I've never felt so protected by the FBI. Take care." He's chuckling by the time he drops his phone into his pocket. "She really thought she'd be able to flip you. You just ruined her entire fucking day."

There was a brief time when I thought she might convince me to turn on Gabriel. That's one mistake I'm glad I didn't make, and one Gabriel never needs to hear about. "Good."

His heated gaze drags over my sweaty frame. "Now, how about you make *my* day better."

Excitement stirs in my belly despite our current situation—in Ava's cartel's compound, surrounded by armed men, Gabriel's once-crisp white shirt stained with his blood. "And how would I go about doing that?"

He pulls me against him, our bodies flush. Between us, his hard length presses against my stomach. "See that pool house over there?" He nods behind me.

I look over my shoulder at the cute little building.

"We could go in there and I could get you out of this dress, and then wrap these thighs around my shoulders and taste—"

Gabriel's phone rings in his pocket and he groans deeply.

"You need to get that." Every time someone calls, all I can think about is my father in solitary, wondering what the hell is going on. Or maybe he's figured it out.

"I do." With a kiss against my lips, he releases me and digs his phone out again. "Yeah? Hey, Stanley." A smile of satisfaction curls his lips. "So, it's confirmed? Navarro?" He adds for my benefit, I'm sure. "Give me a minute?" With a second fleeting kiss—this one against my temple—he moves away to continue his conversation with his PI. While he's told me a lot, I think he's hiding just as much. It doesn't bother me anymore. He's trying to protect me.

And while I don't understand all that's happening, everything seems to be falling into place.

Holding onto that hope, I settle down on the edge and slip my legs into the inviting water. If this were under any other situation, it might feel like a holiday.

A pseudo honeymoon, even.

I snort at the insanity of it all, and brush against a dusty patch on my hem. If Gabriel and I are still going through with this city hall marriage, I guess I'll have to find something else to wear.

"I'm afraid that dress may be beyond saving."

I jump at the sound of Ava's voice. She has changed out of her pantsuit and into a white bikini and coral lace cover up. The combination accentuates her tanned olive skin and her voluptuous curves.

I take a deep, calming breath and then say, "I was just thinking that."

"There's no need to be afraid of me. You are in Gabriel and Caleb's world, and from all that I've heard, they aren't stupid men. They trust you." She sits on the edge of the pool beside me, slipping her legs into the water next to mine. "I would have no reason to hurt you, would I?"

"No." But the fact that she is asking disturbs me.

She collects my wrist, stroking a dainty thumb across my skin where the foundation has worn off. The cuff marks are faintly visible. "But someone had reason. I assume this wasn't from a fun night with Gabriel?"

I hesitate, wondering if I should lie. Something tells me lying to our new "friend" would be a bad idea.

"Vlad Easton had his psychotic hitman kidnap me for leverage to force Gabriel to do his bidding."

She hums. "Vlad's secret weapon. Yes, I've heard about Bane. A dreadful man. No one wants to be on his radar. Or Vlad's, for that matter." Her flawless brow furrows. "How did you get away? Did Gabriel save you from him?" Those curious, dark eyes wander to where Gabriel paces, still talking to Stanley. I see the hunger in them. She's attracted to him. Of course she is. Who wouldn't be?

"No. I killed Bane." I didn't mean to admit that; it just slips out.

Her eyes snap back to me. "*You*?" The shock is genuine.

And I realize that maybe *that*'s why I said it, so I could have the satisfaction of seeing the look on her face when she realizes that I'm not a helpless fool.

"Gabriel couldn't find me, and I knew that if I didn't get away, I probably never would." My voice is unexpectedly calm. "So, I did what I had to in order to survive."

"Don't we all," she murmurs. "Bane was a bad man. He deserved what he got." After a moment she adds, "My father also deserved what he got."

I can't begin to imagine the kinds of atrocities her cartel boss of a father has committed. If it's anything like Bane or Vlad, then, yes, he likely did.

I'm surrounded by people who are actively trying or have already succeeded in killing their fathers. Meanwhile, I ended up in this situation because I was willing to do anything to keep mine alive. The irony of that makes me chuckle, though there's nothing funny about it.

She studies me closely. "Remind me to never underestimate you."

The deep hum of Gabriel's voice pulls my attention to him, and I take a moment to admire the shape of his broad shoulders, the curve of his back, and the swell of his ass in his dress pants. Even in bloodied and torn clothing, he seems powerful, indomitable, in control. But I can't forget those few moments, wrapped in each other's arms, when he showed a vulnerable side, when he admitted to his fears.

There's a notable buoyancy to him now, one that I haven't seen since I've known him. It's almost as if he sees the light at the end of a very long, dark tunnel.

Will this new arrangement with Ava jeopardize his dream of a different life though?

I won't allow it, because it doesn't just affect Gabriel anymore. This is also my life.

"Gabriel wants out and I want him out." I meet Ava's gaze. "Respectfully, after today, I'm hoping I never have a reason to see you again."

She dips her head. "I understand. We didn't meet on the best of terms."

I can't help the snort that escapes.

"Despite that, I am not my father. I don't embrace violence unless it's a last resort. Perhaps I can still change your opinion of me."

Highly unlikely.

Ava looks to the dining area and the man pouring water into glasses nods.

With a clap of excitement, she climbs to her feet. "Time to eat." She sashays toward the terrace, her steps measured and confident, as if she owns the world.

And maybe she will—a world where these dirty empires thrive.

But Gabriel and I will be far away from it.

TWENTY-ONE
GABRIEL

"THIS IS NOT how I saw today going." Caleb inhales the last of his wine—a full-bodied Mexican cabernet produced in Ava's Sonora vineyard.

The second he puts his glass down, a server appears to fill it again.

That's how it's been all afternoon, as we sit on this shaded terrace, the sun slowly sliding across the sky, heading toward evening as Ava plies us with free-flowing liquor and course after course of five-star food—everything from stuffed poblanos to moles, tamales, and carnitas that give Rosita's a run for their money.

The Ava Navarro who stepped out of her white SUV outside Phoenix to threaten our lives this morning has all but vanished, and the one who calmly negotiated our truce is barely recognizable, replaced by this version—a warm and welcoming hostess who jokes often and strikes up conversation easily. Even now, her head is tipped back in throaty laughter over something Vince said.

Caleb leans in to whisper in my ear, "You still think she's gonna try to kill us?"

"Fattening us up for slaughter? Maybe," I murmur wryly around my glass. Despite the tense arrival and the relentless throb in my skull, it didn't take long for me to find my appetite once we sat down. Now, I'm ready to unbuckle my pants. The way Mercy's rubbing her stomach says she feels the same.

Only, I'm not so sure we have anything to fear from Ava—at least not if we hold up our end of the bargain. She sent her entire security team away to station themselves on the outside of the walls—dismissing Tony's objections—and then invited Farley to join us. When Tony tried to relieve him of his gun, she waved it off.

The guy opened his mouth to argue, but all it took was a few sharp words in Spanish and an icy look, and he clamped his mouth shut, fast.

Short answer is, I don't know what the hell to make of Ava Navarro, but by the end of the night, she's either going to try to kill us or fuck us. The way those greedy dark eyes are constantly veering between Caleb and Merrick, my guess is the latter.

My phone rings in my pocket and I tense.

"How long are we gonna keep avoiding that call?" Caleb asks, more somber.

"Until all the dominoes have fallen." I can count the people who've ever had this number on one hand. I doubt it's Donny or Stan calling, because I checked in with them less than an hour ago. I know it's not Bane, for obvious reasons. Eduardo isn't likely to dial this number until after the drop, when all hell breaks loose and he feels the need to remind me that the Eastons are still on the hook for three million dollars.

So there's only one person left. "Let him stew." We're twenty minutes out from the planned drop—a simple handoff of money and truck keys in a parking lot on the southside of the city, entrusted to three of the morons who can't find their assholes in the dark, according to my father—and Vlad wants to know if we're on our way. He may be forcing our hand, but we're merely bobbleheads for him. He thinks he's still running his empire from behind Fulcort's bars.

The ringing stops, only to start up again.

"For fuck's sakes, enough is enough. You need to cut him off *now*," Caleb snaps.

"You know what? You're right." Whatever scheme he was cooking up involving Mercy's father is moot. "Text Donny and tell him to toss his cell."

"With pleasure." Caleb slips out his phone.

Mercy's brow furrows with concern.

"It's all good, babe. Your dad's safer than he's ever been." From what Donny told me, half of Fulcort has already heard that Vlad has no money to pay the sky-high tab he's been running up. It'll be a few hours yet before someone has the balls to ask the old man if it's true.

Vlad Easton may have no damn clue yet that his entire world is crumbling down around him.

"I know." She forces a reassuring smile that doesn't convince either of us.

I can't fault her for that. All I can do is comfort and distract her, something I've been hesitant to do up until now because of this never-ending nightmare I've dragged her into. I reach over and slide a hand over her bare leg. Her skin is warm and soft, and slick from the intense afternoon heat.

The flicker of interest that dances through her gaze tells me she knows where my head is at—or where it wants to be. Between those slender thighs.

"I think I need to go for a walk around the property to digest all this food," I announce, my eyes on her, that pool house and her naked body in the forefront of my dirty mind.

"That sounds like a good idea," she begins to say, but her attention is pulled to Tony and the gun strapped to his hip, as he strolls in.

"Jefa," he addresses Ava—I know enough Spanish to recognize the lady boss title.

"Sí?"

They exchange quick dialogue in Spanish and the easygoing, smiling Ava melts like an ice cube tossed into a fire. Collecting her napkin, she dabs at her lips—the red color painted on them unmarred—her face now stony.

"What's going on?" I steal a wary glance Farley's way.

He senses the shift in her, too. His hand twitches at his side, ready to reach for his gun.

A scuffle of shoes sound inside the house, putting us all instantly on edge. Four guards step out of the house, a bound man stumbling between them.

"This is the part of this business that I have no palate for," Ava says cryptically, standing and gesturing toward the man with her palm up as if serving something to us on a platter. "I promised you retribution for your club manager. Here it is."

Caleb's mouth hangs for several beats. It's so rare to see my brother speechless that, under different circumstances, I'd laugh. "You brought us Mateo Estrada."

"I said I would deliver him to you, didn't I?"

"You did. I just didn't expect it so soon."

"I am a woman of my word. And I couldn't give him time to step into my father's shoes."

Caleb moves fast out of his seat, rounding the table toward Luiz Navarro's righthand man.

The guy's panicked gaze shifts between Caleb and Ava. He looks like a snake, his eyes narrow and flinty, his mouth curved downward. "What have you done, Ava?"

Yeah, I recognize his voice from our brief phone call —when he was all cordial and told me he'd talk Navarro into a sit-down. Now I know he was full of shit; they'd already planned on killing us.

"You didn't think you would be permitted to take on what is rightfully mine, did you?" she says, her tone icy.

We're not stupid. We may *want* Mateo dead, but Ava *needs* him dead so he can't challenge her claim to the cartel empire her father built. Giving him to us means her hands stay relatively clean.

Caleb stops less than a foot away from the guy, towering over him. How this average guy overpowered a guy of Mike's size is beyond me, but a gun barrel against your temple can bring down even the largest of men. "You gonna deny what you did to our friend?"

Mateo pauses as if deciding how to respond. "Which one was your friend?"

"The club manager for Empire."

"Oh, that big bastard." Mateo sneers. He already knows he's a dead man. "He took a little extra work to go down—"

Caleb takes a hard, fast swing and his knuckles collide with Mateo's cheek, snapping the man's head to the side.

He leans over to spit. Blood and several teeth spill to the interlocked stone.

Beside me, Mercy flinches. She's seen far worse than this, but I don't want her to see any more of it.

Thankfully Ava doesn't seem interested either. She fires off instructions in Spanish before waving a hand, and they lead Mateo away, blood dripping down his chin. She takes a long sip of her wine and gingerly sets her glass down in front of her. "Tony will take you and your men to a prepared place. You may bring your guns and deal with him there. But this matter needs to be fully resolved tonight. Is that reasonable?"

Meaning, she doesn't want us going all Bane-like and torturing him under her roof for the next twenty-four hours. That's probably all she knows, being surrounded by the kind of men she's grown up around.

Caleb inhales deeply. If I know my brother at all, adrenaline is coursing through his veins, ready to fuel him for hours. Thankfully his temper won't allow that. Mateo won't last more than twenty minutes before he's full of bullet holes. "More than fair."

I check my watch. "With your father gone and Mateo here, what will happen with our delivery?"

"It's already in motion. The men will still hit it, especially if they believe Vlad is the one behind my father's death."

Then the exchange moves forward as planned.

I brace myself before I look to Mercy, expecting to see everything from disappointment to judgment to disgust for what she's witnessing. After what she went through with Bane, there's no way she'd condone what's about to happen to the guy they just dragged out of here.

Her jaw is tense, and I can't read the look in her eyes, but all she says is, "Do what you need to do and end this tonight."

I nod solemnly. "Farley will stay with you."

Her gaze flickers to the enormous bodyguard. "If you don't need him."

I lean in to plant a kiss on her lips. I've always loved the feel of her mouth against mine. "I need him with you."

We leave the women sitting at the dining table, surrounded by platters and glasses and chairs while we collect retribution for Mike.

Just like our father taught us to do.

THE AIR IS warm and the sun is beginning its descent when I step outside, my phone ringing in my pocket. The shed Ava had prepared is an outbuilding set away from the house and the road and anything resembling normal life. It's used to house farming equipment and landscaping tools for the sizeable fruit orchard in front of me.

Tonight, though, it's draped in plastic for an easy clean-up.

Taking a deep breath, I answer the call.

"Gabriel," a heavily accented male voice curls around my name.

There's only one person this could be and he's an important domino. "Eduardo."

"I assume you are aware of what happened at the exchange?"

"I just got the call." Stanley confirmed that the drop happened as planned.

"I lost two good men," he says evenly, and I can't tell if he's truly upset or is simply posturing over expendable drug runners.

"And we lost three of our own," I counter. Three especially hotheaded guys who I knew wouldn't balk at pulling their guns, which is exactly what I banked on. Afterall, the idiots thought they were getting a big promotion. Now they're three dead idiots who can't ever trade intel on our family.

There's a long pause, as if he's waiting for me to speak. "What a clusterfuck," he mutters after a moment. "Hit by both the DEA *and* Navarro's people? How does that happen?"

"I have no fucking clue how the DEA found out," I lie. Stanley filtered the tip through several layers to get to a known informant. He assured me it'll never blow back to us. "But Navarro's men took out JJ and Ivan on Saturday night and that must be how *they* found out. I warned Vlad that it was too hot—"

"Then why didn't we make alternate arrangements?" Eduardo snaps.

"You know my father. He didn't want to risk losing customers with delays."

"Yes, I know Vlad. He is passionate about his business." Eduardo sighs heavily. "But now he's out his product and double his money, because I still expect to be paid."

There it is. "You'll get your money." Courtesy of the stash houses we cleared out.

"And the next shipment?"

"We won't be taking any more shipments until further notice." As in, forever. "Our networks are crumbling, our manpower being picked off; there's too much volatility right now. This will keep happening."

"You're going completely dry?" There's no mistaking the surprise in his voice. The Eastons don't halt supply. Ever.

"Yes."

"This is Vlad's decision?"

"My father is reckless, as he's just proven. He just cost us six million dollars. He's no longer making decisions for this family."

"So the cubs are finally confronting the lion." There's a long pause. "And Peter—"

"Betrayed our father." I leave it at that. "I'm sure you can find another buyer for your product."

"There are always people to take my product, though I enjoyed the mutually beneficial relationship with your family." He puffs on something—a cigar, is my guess—and I hold my breath as I wait for the next words out of his mouth. Will he make ending this business relationship difficult or easy? That's been the only real wild card in my hand all along "But I can appreciate why you would be hesitant, given all the turmoil I've been hearing about north of the border. And now that Peter is gone and Vlad has lost his magic touch, I also find myself hesitant."

I knew discrediting our father in his eyes would be essential. "Are we good here?"

Two distinctive pops sound from inside the shed, one after another, and I know someone has delivered justice for Mike.

"As long as I get my money."

"It'll be on its way within the hour."

"Then we're good. I wish you well. And maybe our paths will cross one day." Eduardo ends the call, leaving me listening to dead air and feeling the invisible hundred-pound lead weight lift from my chest.

It's done.

Uncle Peter and our cousins, gone.

Navarro, gone.

Bane, gone.

Mercy and her father, safe.

Agent Lewis has no case against us—at least not through Mercy.

Every threat to us has been handled.

All, but one.

The door creaks as Caleb, Merrick, and Vince emerge from the shed.

"I think I broke a knuckle." Caleb holds his bloodied and bruised hands out in front of him as he falls into step beside me, heading back along a path through the orchard toward the house. Tension still radiates off his shoulders. My brother pretends he enjoys exacting revenge, but the truth is he's going to hit the bottle and the powder hard tonight to quiet the voices that tug at his conscience.

"You totally broke a knuckle." Merrick slides a smoke from a pack and tucks it between his lips, before holding the pack out to Caleb. "You want me to teach you how to throw a punch?"

"Yeah, let me practice on your face." Caleb takes a cigarette and then nods to me. "Was that Eduardo?"

I smirk. "Yup. Wants his money."

"That fucking bastard." Caleb chuckles. "I still think we should have moved the drop and gone through with the deal. Now the damn DEA has all our money *and* our coke."

I shake my head. "It's better this way." How would I have looked Mercy in the eye, had I done that? It was one thing when we were reaping the rewards, but I don't ever want her to think of me as a drug dealer. I look to Merrick. "Hey, give us a minute?"

With a brief glance at Caleb, the two Perris move ahead.

"What's wrong now?" Caleb mutters.

"Ava's delivered on everything else she's promised. She's going to follow through on Dad."

"*Oh, Ava.*" He ends that thought on a sigh. "Can't wait to see what's under that little bikini."

I roll my eyes. Leave it to Caleb to go straight to pussy after putting a bullet in someone. "My point is, why do you need to see the old man one more time before this is done?"

Smoke sails from his lips into the evening sky. "I need to see the look on his ugly face the moment he realizes he's lost everything. I've waited years to see that. Don't you want to see that, after all he's put you through?"

"I thought I did. But now, all I want is for it to be over so we can move on with our lives." So I can move on with Mercy.

We walk in oddly peaceful silence, past Ava's men. They nod as we pass. I guess we're not a threat to them anymore, even armed. If I let my ego dwell on that for too long, I might get offended. The Easton name has always meant money, power, and a healthy dose of fearful respect.

We reach the pools just as the property lights kick in, casting an inviting purplish glow over the water. Mercy is floating on her back, wearing a borrowed bathing suit —I assume lent to her by Ava. She looks like a goddess, her raven black hair fanning out around her head.

How quickly that woman has become my heart, my home, my life.

I'll never deserve her, but I'll kill myself trying to change that. That's my new mission in life—being good enough for her.

Our appearance disturbs her drift. She rolls and

repositions, until only her head is visible. Her dark brown eyes scour over us—over Caleb's bloody knuckles, over the gun at my side—and her brow furrows deeply. She may have told me to do what we need to do, but I know her well enough to know that she'll never condone it.

Ava is approaching from the far side, a champagne flute in her hand. She draws every man's attention, except mine.

I watch Mercy's gaze shift from us, to Ava, back to us, and to Caleb's hands again. Abruptly, she turns and swims away, slipping beneath the manmade waterfall and disappearing into the pool cave.

"Been a real fucking rollercoaster these past few days, huh?" Caleb murmurs, watching Mercy vanish.

"It's not over, yet."

Caleb sighs heavily. "You know what? We've spent a lifetime dealing with that hateful fuck. Why would we waste another goddamn minute catering to him and his never-ending bullshit? Why give him a chance to fuck us over again?" Caleb looks to me. "Forget what I said before. This ends tonight."

I take a deep breath. An odd, numbing sensation passes over me. "Tonight."

His eyes rake over Ava's lean, tanned body "I'll tell her to get it done."

Ava stops a few feet away, halfway between Caleb and Merrick. "I'm glad that dirty business is finished." Her red-painted lips settling onto the rim of her glass as she takes a dainty sip.

"Seems like all your plans went off without a hitch." And dove-tailed perfectly into ours.

She dips her head. "So far, yes. Tomorrow, I'll fly back to Hermosillo to tie up some loose ends. And then I'll be in contact with you all to sort out details, stateside. If you'd like to leave, I think it's safe now. At your leisure, of course."

"I think Mercy's ready to sleep in her own bed," I admit. And so am I.

"Not before I collect that drink Ava promised," Caleb drawls, offering her a roguish smile, one that pops those deep dimples women seem to melt over.

She answers with a secretive smile. "Did I promise a drink?"

Caleb smiles. "I'm sure of it."

Ava tsks, collecting his bloody hand in hers.

"It's fine. Nothing some soap and ice can't fix."

"I have plenty of both inside. If you need a second helicopter, my pilot will gladly take you wherever you wish to." She says this to me, and I hear her meaning loud and clear: "If you and Mercy want to leave while I let your brother violate every orifice in my body, here, take my ride."

"If you'll follow me." She begins walking toward a set of double glass doors, expecting Caleb to follow.

"Give me an hour and then I'll head back with you guys." He's talking to me, but his eyes are on her ass.

"An hour?"

"Yeah. Go for a swim."

I just want to go home, but I'm not leaving this idiot

here to get cut up into pieces by Ava's men because he does something to make her angry. "An hour."

Merrick quietly falls into line behind Ava, stealing a glance Caleb's way.

The tiny smile that curls my brother's lips tells me he was hoping for this turn of events. "Maybe two."

Vince, also seeing where this celebratory drink is heading, hangs back, digging his phone out. "I've got some calls to make."

"Cale…" With all the blood rushing to his dick, there's a good chance he's already forgotten what we just agreed on.

"Fine. An hour. It's all I ask." He turns to walk backward toward the house, nodding toward the pool. "Go on and celebrate, 'cause it ends tonight." He gives me a knowing look before disappearing into the house.

TWENTY-TWO
MERCY

THE TRANQUIL SOUND of the waterfall muffles out all sound from the outside world.

Which is exactly what I was hoping for when I slipped into this little cave and crawled up on the ledge in a nook. I don't want to see or hear details about that man's murder, whether he deserved it or not. There's no question Caleb beat him—the evidence is all over his fists.

But what part did Gabriel play? Is he the one who shot him?

I shudder. Half of me wants the answer; the other half never wants to think about this day ever again.

"Mercy?" Gabriel calls out, a second before he appears through the waterfall.

Despite my trepidation, my heart begins to flutter at the sight of him. He's stripped down to nothing. "Should you even be in a pool? Those stitches are fresh."

"There's a lot of things I probably shouldn't be

doing." He swims up to where I'm perched, pushing my thighs apart to fit his torso in between. He hooks his thumbs through the strings in my bikini bottom but doesn't attempt to tug them off, seemingly content to rest his chin on my thigh.

When the newest Navarro cartel leader handed me the black bikini, the last thing I felt like doing was swimming, until I dove into the salt water.

"We good?" he asks softly.

I push a wet strand of hair off his forehead. "Of course we're good."

A dark cloud passes across his gaze. "I never wanted you to see any of this."

"I know." But I signed up for it when I took his deal, whether I realized it or not.

"It's almost done."

"Vlad?"

"Being taken care of as we speak." His eyes flip to me, and the meaning there is clear.

His father will be dead soon.

I take a shaky breath. "I thought you guys wanted to see him one more time." Caleb said as much in Ava's office.

"I don't want to see anyone but you, not worrying about your father or me or yourself anymore." Gabriel presses his lips against my skin. "That's all that matters to me anymore. You're all that matters to me."

I stroke my fingers through his hair, careful of the wound. "Will Ava let us go home now? It's been a very long day and I'm tired."

"Yeah, we're all done here. We're just waiting for Caleb."

"What's he doing?"

"Ava." He smirks. "And maybe Merrick."

"Oh my God. Of course." I chuckle, but in my mind—in the far distance, obscured by the horrifying memory of Bane—I recall a heady night overlooking the Vegas rooftop terrace, with Caleb and Merrick swapping women under the night sky.

Caleb, Ava, and Merrick though…. That's a different dynamic. I'm not sure how that will work. "Are they out there?" I nod toward the pools.

"No. They're in the house. She's the boss of a cartel now. She probably shouldn't do things like that in front of her men." Gabriel traces a playful fingertip over my bare skin, slipping beneath the seam of my bikini bottom. Gooseflesh instantly prickles my bare skin, with the anticipation of him slipping that fingertip inside and teasing me the way he so expertly does.

Only, he stops short, as if thinking better of it, and then slips his hand back out.

My frustration swells. I know he's trying to be respectful—of my ordeal the last few days, of the fact that we're in a cartel compound surrounded by security—but right now I need the Gabriel I know back. "If you see Gabriel Easton anywhere, can you return him to me, please? You know, the dirty, foul-mouthed bastard I met at Fulcort?" On impulse, I reach down and yank the ties of my bikini, unfastening the bottoms. The material falls off.

His eyebrow arches.

We have an hour to kill in here, and no one can see us, hidden within this little nook. The thrill of that is stirring my blood. I lean back against the wall and pull my thighs apart.

With a curse and a devilish smirk, he dives in.

I sigh with the first swipe of his tongue. "*There* he is."

"ARE WE *FINALLY* READY TO GO?" Caleb hollers as we exit the pool house, hand in hand, dressed in our ruined clothes.

Gabriel makes a point of checking his watch. Three hours have past since he swam through that waterfall. We spent most of it in the king-sized bed, planning our future between rounds of slow, mind-blowing sex. Meanwhile, Vince found a comfortable spot on a lounger where he drifted off, waiting for his brother's exploits to wrap up.

He and Merrick head toward their helicopter with no more than a nod toward us, as if to say, "Until next time." Merrick's hair is mussed and his lips are puffy, and he wears a small smile as if carrying a secret.

"Thanks for the drink." Caleb blows a kiss to Ava, who watches us from a second-floor balcony, her silky black robe rustling in the slight breeze. "We'll be in touch soon about that hotel. I could use your help getting him to come around!" His eyes are red and bleary, and I doubt that's just from booze, knowing Caleb and his proclivity for recreational drugs.

Will he ever outgrow this reckless lifestyle?

"Perhaps." Ava's dark eyes drift to me. With a nod, she disappears into the house.

And we head for the gates.

Gabriel wraps his arms around me as we watch Merrick and Vince's helicopter take off into the night sky, heading toward Napa.

"When do you think we'll see them again?"

"Sooner than I want, I'm sure." Gabriel's eyes are on Ava's pilot as he climbs into the other helicopter and starts the engine.

"But not too soon."

"No, babe, not too soon." He nuzzles his face into the crook of my neck. "We have a few things we need to take care of. A visit to city hall in the morning, a trip to Saint Lucia in the afternoon…."

A thrill courses through me. I've already booked the week off and with Empire closed, there's no better time for the two of us to escape. "After a visit to your doctor for your head, of course."

He groans. "Of course."

Gabriel's phone rings, and his body instantly tenses against mine. I've come to know the different phones and their ringtones. This is the phone he uses for calls he doesn't ever want traced back to him.

He promised me that my father would be safe, and yet I hold my breath as he answers, as he speaks in a low murmur to the person on the line, as he turns away from me. As he finally ends the call.

Caleb and I are both watching intently—I think, for very different reasons.

"That was Donny," Gabriel confirms after a moment.

My stomach drops. "And?"

Gabriel swallows, his eyes flipping to his brother. "It's done."

"Done," Caleb echoes, his complexion paling a few shades as the shock of the news that their father is dead hits him. "Wow. It's really… For real?"

Gabriel slides his phone into his pocket. "Yeah."

"How?"

"Does it matter?"

Caleb seems to consider that. "No. I guess it doesn't. Not tonight, anyway."

Silence hangs over them as they process the news that the man who has caused them—and countless others—so much grief and fear will never harm anyone else ever again.

"Are you okay?" I ask, because I don't know what the hell else to say.

Gabriel tips his head back and releases a long exhale. "It's finally over. We're free."

"Ready for takeoff when you are!" The pilot hollers from the open door.

"Yeah, we're ready!" Caleb heads for his seat as the blades begin to churn.

Gabriel reaches for me. "Let's go home."

I don't hesitate, diving into his arms.

EPILOGUE

Mercy

One year later…

The front door shuts with a thud, announcing Gabriel's return home. "Caleb's flying in early. He'll be here in an hour."

"What?" I shriek, nearly dropping the Betty Crocker chocolate cake I've been icing for the past hour. "No! We had a deal! He's not allowed here tonight."

The second Gabriel rounds the corner and I see those dimples on display, I know he's joking. "That's not funny!" I toss an oven mitt at his head.

He dives to the right, barely missing it. "I'm sorry, babe. I couldn't help it." He's laughing. "But he is coming in tomorrow, for a few days."

"Doesn't he have a hotel and casino to run?" I

mutter. A month after that tryst with Merrick and Ava, Gabriel got a call from Bruce Cohen, asking if he was still interested in buying the Mage. I don't know if it was a visit from a Mexican cartel boss or the fact that Cohen landed in bed with a sixteen-year-old call girl and Merrick "conveniently" captured video footage of it, but the deal went down, with Merrick and Vince buying up the other partners' shares. Since then, Caleb's been spending most of his time in Vegas, bickering with Merrick and trying to screw his manager. But every few weeks, I'll come downstairs and find him stretched out on the couch in our living room, usually dressed but not always.

Gabriel shrugs. "He misses us."

That or he needs a break from the stress of running a Vegas hotel and casino. Either way, he's still a pig, but he's become an endearing one to me.

I sigh. "Tomorrow, I can deal with. But tonight has to be perfect. Which means no Caleb." It's my father's first night free of Fulcort since Justin had his conviction overturned. It's taken nearly a year and he's not completely free and clear yet, but Justin's confident that by the time he's done with the justice system, Dad will never have to see another day inside any prison walls.

Gabriel leans in to kiss me and I inhale his delicious woodsy cologne. He left early this morning for Empire so he could get urgent work done in time to be home for the drive to Fulcort. Finding a suitable replacement for Mike hasn't been easy, even now that the club runs fully legit—no laundering of anything but VIP tablecloths.

"Come on, how bad could it be? Your dad's finally coming around with me."

"Yeah, I don't know if I'd call it *that*, exactly." By the time I sat down across from him and fessed up, he'd already heard. Apparently gossip runs through a prison faster than it does in a high school. What he hadn't heard—what no one knew yet—was that he now had a son-in-law.

To say he wasn't pleased would be an understatement.

Thankfully, Dad's never been one to hold a grudge.

"Well, he's stuck with me for good." Gabriel drops to his knees to press his lips against my swollen belly—a daily ritual he has with his daughter that makes my heart ache with adoration. She was a surprise that we certainly didn't plan for, but now that she's coming, I already can't imagine life without her.

"Marsha got the check."

"Oh yeah? What's she putting in? A pool? Sauna?"

I snort. "Shut up. She's actually looking at building a small addition so they can have a yoga and meditation studio."

"That sounds useful."

"I think it will be. I'm sure the counselors will appreciate it as much as the clients." I know I would, if I still worked there. I decided to leave Mary's Way soon after we married. While I love Gabriel and don't regret the path I've chosen for my life, I couldn't work there anymore, given the ties I have to this world, even in the past. Maybe I'll return one day.

Marsha's not dumb; she knows who I'm married to,

and she has a good idea how Gabriel amassed his fortune. When I brought the first check, she wanted to refuse it until I convinced her to see it under a different light.

A way to make amends for the harm Vlad Easton caused so many families.

Now we meet for lunch once a month. She tells me about the latest happenings around the clinic and I slide a sizeable donation across the table.

Gabriel opens the fridge and pulls out a beer. "What did Rosita make for dinner?"

"Why do you assume Rosita's making dinner?"

"Because you said so yourself, tonight's special. And because I've tasted your cooking and your father has had enough of prison food."

I burst out laughing.

His deep chuckle joins in as his arms curl around my waist, his hand cupping a breast. Of all my growing assets, he's appreciated those most. "How long before we have to leave for Fulcort?"

"Twenty minutes?"

He leans over to capture my fingertip in his mouth, sucking off the smear of chocolate icing. "That'll do."

Did you enjoy Fallen Empire?

If so, please consider leaving a review.

THE WOLF HOTEL, SNEAK PEEK

Have you met Henry Wolf Yet? Enjoy this excerpt from Tempt Me, Book One in the Wolf Hotel Series

One

February

"I didn't mean for it to happen, Abigail. I swear!"

"You didn't mean for it to happen! You didn't mean to put your..." My words fall apart with my sobs. I can barely see Jed's face through my tears. Tears that haven't stopped since I ran for my dorm room earlier today. Tears that have left my skin raw and tight. And every time I think I'm all cried out, the image of Jed and *her* flashes inside my head and a fresh wave hits.

I wipe my dripping nose against my sweatshirt sleeve. I'm far past the point of caring what I look like. "Who is she, anyway?"

"Nobody important." He brushes his own tears

away with his palm and then reaches for my face, cupping my cheeks. "You are my whole life. You've *always* been my whole life. Always! You know that, right? Tell me you know that!"

I swallow against the sharp knot lodged in my throat but it doesn't budge. I *knew* that. Up until today. "Then why would you break my heart?"

His handsome face flinches as if I'd slapped him. Something I wish I had the nerve to do. "You weren't supposed to find out."

Oh my God! "That makes it better?"

"No, that's not what I'm saying." He hangs his head for a moment. "Look, we're getting married next year and then it's just you and me. It's been just you and me for *all* these years. And," he swallows, hesitates, "this is something I've been thinking about. A lot, lately."

"About cheating on me?"

"No! About, you know..." He winces. "Sex."

That's what this is all about? "Why didn't you tell me? I would have—"

"No, Abigail." Jed's face is suddenly stern. "You and me, we're doin' it the right way by waiting until we're man and wife. You're so innocent. So pure." He leans forward, pressing his forehead against mine. "It means everything to me that you'll give that to me on our wedding night. But"—a sheepish look overtakes his face—"I'm a guy. It's different for me."

"How is it different?" Who is this person sitting in front of me?

"Because we're weak! This is something I need to do. I need to get this out of my system, or I'm afraid I'll make a mistake down the road, when it *really* matters. Trust me on this one. You don't want me straying later on, when we have kids, do you?"

I'm listening, but I'm not believing these words coming out of Jed's mouth. "So we're breaking up?"

"No." He frowns. "Not exactly. We're taking a little breather, okay? Just until I can get my head on straight. But we're meant to be, you and me." He brushes strands of hair off my face, like he's done a thousand times. "I'll come back to you. I promise."

I'm so angry and hurt, I can't even face him anymore, so I fix my eyes on the small gumball machine promise ring he gave me on my sixteenth birthday, my sobs drowning out the rest of his words.

April

"Look directly into the camera when you answer the questions," the woman commands, her cold blue irises piercing behind a pair of trendy horn-rimmed glasses. Between those, her honey-blonde bun, the fitted black business suit and four-inch heels, she could pass for one of those librarian/strippers instead of a corporate recruiter.

I adjust my practical gold-wire-framed round spectacles. "Okay."

She readies the iPhone sitting in the stand for taping while I fidget on my stool, tucking wayward strands of my ginger hair behind my ear and smoothing the wrinkles from my shirt. I didn't come dressed for a videotaped interview. I figured this job fair would be like any other; I'd wander by some basic booths, collect a few pamphlets, and talk to representatives who want to be anywhere but a Chicago library on a Saturday.

For the most part, that's what it is. But the booth for Wolf Hotels is different. It's three times the size as of the others, with sharply-dressed recruiters and an on-site interviewing station behind a screen, to help speed up the hiring process for those who meet the basic criteria.

And the only reason I made the basic criteria is because I lied on the paper application that I filled out twenty minutes ago. Now I'm petrified of getting caught.

"Full name, please."

I've always hated being on camera. I clear my throat nervously. "Abigail Mitchell. But I go by Abbi," I'm quick to add. My mama calls me Abigail, and everyone else from my hometown calls me Abigail because of my mama. I've never liked it.

The interviewer is stone-faced. She doesn't care what I go by. "The role that you're applying for?"

"Outdoor Maintenance and Landscaping?" I think that was the official title on the application form.

"And please describe your experience that will be invaluable to us, Abigail."

"It's Abbi." I force my biggest smile and hope my annoyance doesn't show on video when they play it back later. "Sure. Well, first off, I love the outdoors. I grew up on a farm and have spent years baling hay, throwing bags of grain, and hauling buckets of water for the animals. So don't worry, I'm plenty strong." People don't believe that I am. My slim five-foot-five stature is deceiving, but one look at my body in shorts and a tank will attest that I'm feminine but honed with muscle from long days on the Mitchell farm.

I've already provided all of this information on the handwritten application form, but I guess they want the live version as well. "I've run my own landscaping company for five years, operating out of Greenbank, Pennsylvania, maintaining commercial properties with excellence." I've been pulling dandelions and cutting grass around my podunk town every summer since I was fourteen. To call what I do "landscaping" is a farce. But if it gets me this job, far the hell away from my life, I'll say anything.

"Were any of these properties hotels?"

"Yes." Never say "no" in an interview. Always find a way to spin it into a yes.

"Please tell me about these hotels."

Crap. And there it is. I've never been a good liar. "It was just one, actually. It's called the Inn. It's...an upscale bed-and-breakfast." Three rooms in an old Victorian house, run by Perry and Wendy Rhodes. I hear one of the rooms is decorated with a cat theme. Cat wallpaper, cat pillows. Cats, everywhere.

By the way the woman's painted red lips are pressed together, I'm pretty sure my answer is not the one she was looking for. "Okay. Thank you. I also see here that you worked weekends serving customers at a place called the Pearl for several years."

"Yes. That's my aunt's restaurant. I'd help her out during the busy season." I hesitated about using Aunt

May as a reference. I can't be sure she'll give me a glowing recommendation if it means I won't be coming back to Greenbank for the summer. Mama would have her skin if she ever found out she helped make that happen.

"What type of establishment is it?"

"A family restaurant."

"So, not fine dining?"

I sigh. "No. I wouldn't call it that." Slapping together hot turkey sandwiches and pouring Cokes from a fountain does not make for fine dining.

"And have you ever cleaned houses professionally... No," she says, seeing me shake my head fervently, my face twisting with disdain at even the suggestion. That means dealing with fitted sheets all day long, and that sounds like torture to me.

"I see you've also done receptionist work."

Finally, something I can answer truthfully and positively. "Yes. I've worked part-time in my church's office for years. I still do, when I go home for the summer."

"What exactly did you do for them?"

"Answer phones and schedule appointments for the Reverend. I also balance the church's books and organize the annual Corn Roast weekend charity BBQ for our parish." Something I can't bring myself to do again this summer, but will be guilted into doing by my mama and the reverend, should I go back to Greenbank.

She scans my application. "I see you're in school right now." She pauses, and I realize that I'm supposed to answer her.

"Yes. I have one more year in a Bachelor of Arts

degree." The right side of my face is burning from the heat of the lamp. I imagine this is what an interrogation feels like. How much longer is this going to take?

"Are you able to commit to the four-month contract, from May through August?"

"North Gate College starts in September and exams finish at the end of this month, so that won't be a problem."

She smiles. "Good. And what are your plans for after college, Abbi?"

My face falls before I'm able to control my expression. That question catches me off guard. She's talking about next summer, and all I can focus on is getting through today, tomorrow, and this summer. Ideally in Alaska.

Is this where I'm supposed to lie and say that I aspire for a career with Wolf Hotels? I debate my answer for a few heartbeats, and finally decide on the truth. "Honestly, I'm not sure anymore. I was supposed to get married and help run the family farm, but my fiancé and I are—" I stop myself with a deep breath and then an embarrassed little smile. So inappropriate for an interview. "My personal situation is in limbo," I say instead, my voice growing husky, my eyes burning with the threat of tears. It's all still too fresh, too raw. "I'll probably go back home. My family's there."

"And help run the farm?" Her eyes graze over me—over my thick braid that I can't help but toy with when I'm nervous, over my favorite royal-blue button-down that's probably been washed one too many times, over my generic jeans, and down to my Converse—and I know she's judging me. I sit up straighter, feeling more self-conscious than I already do being in front of a camera.

I look nothing like her, or any of the other recruiters here. They're all put together, with smooth, richly colored hair and perfectly painted faces. I don't wear much makeup; just a little lip gloss and, on occasion, shimmery pink nail polish. I don't use hairspray and not a drop of dye has ever touched my hair for fear that it'll make the color worse than it already is.

"Yes." That has always been the plan. But now I feel like I need to defend myself. I'm not just another farm girl, getting ready to bake pies and pop out little farm babies. "I started a side business making soaps, moisturizers, and essential oils a few years back. It's called Sage Oils. I'm going to focus on expanding that." Sage, after my favorite herb, though my products involve everything from mint to lavender to lemon. Up until this point, the bulk of my sales have been thanks to the annual Christmas bazaar and summer fair. I can't complain though; that money will pay for my flight to Homer, should Wolf hire me.

"My, you're quite the enterprising young woman. And so busy. Landscaping and soapmaking businesses, college, farming..." I can't read the woman's tone to tell if she's genuinely impressed. "And what do you do for enjoyment, Abbi?"

I bite my bottom lip to stop myself from saying "Umm" while I think. Wolf Hotels is one of the most posh lines of hotels in the world. I need to sound smart if I have a hope in hell of getting this job. "As you have noted, I'm quite busy with work and school. When I have free time, I spend it with my family, and with my church, solidifying my faith." Which is in some dicey water as of late. "I also volunteer at the local animal shelter, both here in Chicago as well as at home."

"So you like animals?"

"Yes!" I nod emphatically. "I'm excited to see Alaska's wilderness."

She offers me a tight smile. "Right. Last question. Why should we hire you to work at Wolf Cove in Alaska?"

I look down at the pamphlet in my hand—pictures of white-capped mountains and vast wilderness, glacier valleys and volcanoes.

Thousands of miles of serenity, of nothingness.

Thousands of miles from my current life.

They don't want to listen to my sob story, and it's sure as hell not going to get me hired. I struggle to smile as I stare into the camera, silently pleading with my eyes to whoever is making the hiring decisions. "Because I'm smart, hardworking, diligent, and ethical. I respect people and I love a challenge. Plus, I've always wanted to visit Alaska, and this looks like an incredible once-in-a-lifetime opportunity." I clear my throat. "I have nothing to distract my focus. I will give Wolf Cove *everything* I have to offer this summer."

She presses a button and steps around. "Great. Thank you. We'll be in touch."

"When will you be making your decisions?" It's the beginning of April; I'd be flying out in four weeks if I get hired.

"Shortly. We've already filled many of the positions from our pool of current Wolf employees who are interested in the Alaska location. We're just plugging some last-minute holes with outside recruitment." She sticks my application into a red file folder. Is that the reject file?

"Do I have a chance? Honestly." I can't believe I asked that, but I have nothing left to lose.

"We tend to hire people who already have luxury hotel chain experience. But we'll be in touch." She stands there with her arm leading the way to the exit.

My shoulders sag. I force myself to leave before I beg her to put in a good word for me.

There's no way I'm getting this job.

May

I inhale deeply, reveling in the crisp ocean air as land approaches ahead. Chicago was in the seventies when I left this morning. Two layovers, a flight delay, and fifteen hours later, the fifty-five degree day's high has dipped to low forties and I had to dig my winter jacket out of my suitcase.

"Have you ever been to Alaska before?" the captain, a soft-spoken white-haired man named John asks, his hands resting easily on the ferry's wheel.

I shake my head, my gaze drifting over the sea of evergreen and rock as far as the eye can see. We left the dock in Homer thirty minutes ago. It didn't seem like it would take that long to cross, but Kachemak

Bay is vast and wide and unlike anything I've ever seen.

And on the other side of it is my home for the next four months.

I'm so glad I remembered to pop an Antivert an hour before boarding. I'd be puking over the rails by now had I not. Boats and I have never coexisted well.

"So, what made you come?" I can tell John likes to talk, as much for conversation as to assess the foreigners coming to his homeland.

"A brochure," I answer simply, honestly.

He chuckles. "Yeah, it'll do that, all right. Lures plenty of folk our way."

I smile, though his words resonate deep inside. It "lured" me. Yes, that's exactly what it did.

Frankly, the brochure didn't need to work too hard.

When things take an ugly turn, people are always saying they're going to pick up and move far away. Australia, France, anywhere that puts an ocean between them and their problems. Most don't ever act on that. I certainly had no intention of doing so.

And then I went to that job fair in the city library, more than a little panicked about what I was going to do this summer. Recruiters were peddling administrative and counselor positions, trade internships, day care. Nothing I was interested in. Plus, they were all local Chicago-based positions. The last thing I wanted to do was stay in Chicago for the summer. I needed to separate myself from it and its bitter memories, if for only a few months until school started again in the fall.

But the idea of going back to Pennsylvania, where

everyone including the cows had heard the nitty-gritty details about my breakup with Jed, was even more unappealing.

That's what happens when you grow up in a small town and then go away to college with your high school sweetheart, who's also the reverend's son, who you were supposed to marry the summer after you both graduate college.

Who you've been saving yourself for.

Who you caught with his pants down and thrusting into some raven-haired jezebel.

And, while in the depths of despair, though you know better, you tell your upstanding, churchgoing mama, who is known around town as much for her raspberry pie as for her big mouth.

That scandal sure gave the folks of Greenbank something to talk about during Pennsylvania's long, cold winter. It's been months since D-Day, or what I like to call Dick Day, when I caught him. February 2, to be exact.

I'm sure tongues were wagging across pews during church service. When I visited over Easter weekend though, I got nothing but sympathetic nods and pats. Jed, sitting in the pew directly across from us, earned more than a few glowers. Not everyone shared those feelings, though. His father, Reverend Enderbey, decided that giving a sermon on man's weakness for carnal flesh and the need for forgiveness and understanding would be more appropriate than discussing the resurrection of Christ that day.

Much like Jed promised me, Reverend Enderbey has

promised my parents that this is just a momentary blip in Jed's faith; that he's feeling confused and needs to sort out his priorities. He'll come back to me, after he's done sowing his wild oats.

Why do they all think I'll want to take him back?

He broke my heart that day, and has continued breaking it daily, every time I see him walking hand in hand around campus with *her*.

He's not just sowing wild oats. They're *dating* now.

So when I passed by the Wolf Hotels booth at the job fair a month ago and spotted the pamphlet with a beautiful vista of snow-capped mountains and forest, I immediately stopped and started asking questions, and within ten minutes I knew that Wolf Cove was my ticket away from sadness, temporarily at least. I just needed to get myself to Homer, Alaska. They'd provide transportation to the hotel, subsidized accommodations and meals onsite, and weekly transport to Homer, if needed, and in turn I'd work like a dog and keep my mind occupied.

The best part? It was almost 3,800 miles from everything I know.

It sounded perfect. And unattainable. I walked out of that interview feeling hopeless, assuming that there was no way I'd get the job.

And yet I'm standing here today. I call that divine intervention. God knew I needed this miracle.

It came in the form of a phone call a week after the interview, with an official offer for a position in the Landscaping and Maintenance crew. I screamed. I even shed a few happy tears, which was a nice change from all the sad tears I've spilled since February. Knowing that I could avoid Greenbank, Jed, and my family, that I would be leaving my dorm room the day after my last exam and hopping onto a plane… that's the only reason I've held it together this long.

The ferry turns left to run along the coastline, farther into the bay.

"What are those places, over there? Do people live out here?" I point toward the little huts speckling the shore, camouflaged within the trees.

"Nah. They're mostly lodges and cabin rentals."

I study the structures, like yurts on stilts overlooking the water. "They're nice. Rustic."

"They are, indeed."

"Not like Wolf Cove, though."

John chuckles softly, shaking his head. "Not quite."

If the pictures in the pamphlet are at all accurate. My mama's convinced that it's all computer generated, that nothing that luxurious would exist up in Alaska. That I'll end up contracting West Nile from the thick fog of mosquitoes, or I'll wake up in the rickety shack that I'm sleeping in to find a bear gnawing on my leg.

To say Bernadette Mitchell is unhappy about this Alaska job is an understatement. At first she flat-out told me that I wasn't allowed to go. I hung up the phone on her that night, the first time I'd ever done that. Probably the first time *anyone's* ever had the nerve to hang up on a woman like her. I half expected her to drive the nine hours and slap me upside the head.

Two days later, after she'd cooled off, she called and tried to persuade me. I was making a grave mistake, leaving Greenbank and Jed. We'd be away from the chaos of Chicago and the temptations that made Jed stray. We'd have each other, day in and day out, and I could remind him of why we're so perfect together.

I know it's not going to be that simple.

So I dug my heels in. I've been "good girl Abbi" all my life, sitting next to my parents at church service every Sunday, keeping company with like-minded people, staying away from the "bad kids" who drank and smoked pot and had sex. Always listening to Mama.

Maybe if I'd just spread my legs for Jed, my heart wouldn't have been smashed into a thousand pieces.

While she's my mama and I know she wants what's best for me, she, too, thinks that Jed and I belong together, and that our reunion is inevitable, once he gets "the devil" out of his system. I had to bite my tongue before I pointed out to her that the girl currently sucking Jed's dick is a significant obstacle in this imminent reconciliation of ours.

I scan the approaching buildings, my excitement triumphing over my exhaustion. "Where is it?"

"Wolf Cove is just around the bend."

Wolf Cove Hotel in Wolf Cove, Alaska. "How do you go about renaming a cove, anyway?"

John chuckles softly again. He's such a pleasant man. "The cove has been Wolf Cove for hundreds of years now. The Wolf family has a lot of history up here, with the gold mines. That's where they made their first fortune. Though I'm sure they could afford to have it renamed, if it came to that. They're a successful lot. Generous, too."

Man, to be a part of that family. They must have a

lot of money, to risk opening a location like this all the way up here, and set their employees up the way they're doing for us, and all the benefits. "Hey, thanks for coming back for me. I didn't want to stay in a motel." It's just John and me on the ferry, and a deck full of crates and supplies. He was kind enough to make another trip across the bay and pick me up after my flight delay. Apparently he carted a full load of college-aged employees over hours ago.

"We didn't want to leave you stranded. 'Specially on the first day. I woulda had to come back for the supplies first thing in the morning, anyway."

I glance at my watch with dismay. "I've missed the orientation session." It started at seven, almost an hour ago. The skies are deceptively light for this time of evening. "I can't believe how bright it still is."

"Wait 'til June."

"Less than five hours of darkness on the equinox, right?"

He grins. "Someone's been doin' her homework."

"I like to be prepared." The day I applied for the job, I ran home and researched Alaska late into the night instead of studying for my exams. The further I dug, the more excited I became, and the harder I prayed that I'd get the job.

"Well, I'm sure one of the ladies will be kind enough to fill you in on what you missed. They seemed like a nice group. Polite youngsters like yourself, for the most part anyway."

At twenty-one, it feels strange to be referred to as a

"youngster," but I guess next to John, who's got to be pushing seventy, that's exactly what I am.

The ferry rounds the crop of small islands and turns toward the cove. John points to the massive building ahead. "And there's Wolf Cove Hotel."

My eyes widen. "Whoa. The brochure pictures weren't fake." And they don't do this place justice.

John chuckles again. "No, they certainly weren't."

I stare at it quietly, mesmerized. The main lodge towers over the water. Even from this distance, I can see that the lodge is grandiose in its design and massive in size. I can't make out the details to appreciate it yet, but there's no doubt it's something to be admired.

"They just made the finishing touches two weeks ago. Been working on it for almost three years, now."

"Is it still opening on Sunday?" Belinda, the woman who called to formally hire me, said that these first few days would be focused on training and last-minute preparations.

"I'll be ferrying in the first guests at noon. I've been bringin' employees in by the boatload over the last two days. There are a lot of you. A high staff-to-guest ratio, I heard someone say."

"How is the Wolf family going to make any money?"

"I'm guessing the twelve-hundred-dollar-a-night price tag will help."

My mouth drops open. "Who can afford that?" I barely scraped together the eleven hundred I needed for my plane ticket here.

"What's that famous line from that movie? Oh, shucks. You may be too young to remember. The one with the baseball and all those cornfields. 'If you build it...'"

I smile. It's only my dad's favorite movie.

He winks.

We fall into a comfortable silence as we approach, and I realize that I've been rolling my promise ring around my finger unconsciously this entire time. It's been three months since Jed and I broke up and I haven't been able to bring myself to remove it. Now, I slip it off, letting the cheap metal rest in the palm of my hand. A part of me—the hurt, angry part—wants to toss it into the water and be done with it. A symbol of my faith in Jed.

But I can't bring myself to do it just yet. So, I slip the ring into my pocket and try to focus on the months to come.

Meet Henry Wolf now

ALSO BY K.A. TUCKER

The Wolf Hotel Series:

Tempt Me (#1)

Break Me (#2)

Teach Me (#3)

Surrender To Me (#4)

Empire Nightclub Series:

Sweet Mercy (#1)

Gabriel Fallen (#2)

Dirty Empire (#3)

Fallen Empire (#4)

For Contemporary Romance, Women's Fiction, and Romantic Suspense by K.A. Tucker, visit katuckerbooks.com

ABOUT THE AUTHOR

K.A. Tucker writes captivating stories with an edge.

She is the internationally bestselling author of the Ten Tiny Breaths and Burying Water series, He Will Be My Ruin, Until It Fades, Keep Her Safe, The Simple Wild, Be the Girl, and Say You Still Love Me. Her books have been featured in national publications including USA Today, Globe & Mail, Suspense Magazine, Publisher's Weekly, Oprah Mag, and First for Women.

K.A. Tucker currently resides in a quaint town outside of Toronto.

Learn more about K.A. Tucker and her books at katuckerbooks.com

www.ingramcontent.com/pod-product-compliance
Ingram Content Group UK Ltd.
Pitfield, Milton Keynes, MK11 3LW, UK
UKHW041045211025
8505UKWH00009B/94

9 781990 105487